"We Got Too M...
Faro Said. . . .

In a moment they did not, and were grappling, then securely joined, on the sun-dried, pungent grass under the tree. Faro felt the sun bite on his back and legs through the sparse shade of the tree; Mehitabel, under him, was like a pool of cool water to him, warm and vital though she was. He felt no urgency to complete the act, but a desire to prolong its lazy delight.

Dust fountained six feet away, and the flat clap of a rifle shot sounded an instant later. Faro paused in mid-thrust and glared desperately around. The tree that shaded them was too puny to offer shelter, and the nearest rock of any size was over a hundred yards off. There was nowhere to hide. It was fight it out where he was, or nothing.

"What . . . ?" Mehitabel said faintly.

"Stay still," Faro muttered, and grabbed the rifle. . . .

If this don't work, I won't be dying with my boots on, he thought, nor nothing else.

Books by Zeke Masters

Ace in the Hole
The Big Gamble
Bottom Deal
Diamond Flush
Four of a Kind
Luck of the Draw
Riverboat Showdown
Threes Are Wild

Published by POCKET BOOKS

#8

A ZEKE MASTERS WESTERN

ACE IN THE HOLE

PUBLISHED BY POCKET BOOKS NEW YORK

Another *Original* publication of POCKET BOOKS

POCKET BOOKS, a Simon & Schuster division of
GULF & WESTERN CORPORATION
1230 Avenue of the Americas, New York, N.Y. 10020

ISBN: 0-671-42619-2

First Pocket Books printing August, 1981

10 9 8 7 6 5 4 3 2 1

POCKET and colophon are trademarks of Simon & Schuster.

Printed in the U.S.A.

ACE IN THE HOLE

CHAPTER 1

The woman sitting facing Faro Blake inside the Deadwood stage glanced at him boldly, yet with a sly, amused glint in her dark eyes.

"There's just you and me here alone, and it's a long ride," she murmured. "Any ideas about how to pass the time?"

Faro drew on his thin cigar, expelled a cloud of aromatic smoke, and said, "Alone?" with a gesture toward the ungainly blue-clad figure that was slumped against a corner of the coach next to the woman.

"Dead drunk," the woman said. "He wouldn't wake up, no matter what. And what if he did? Expect he'd arrest us, or blacken our reputations? He's fast asleep, all right. Question is, are you?"

"Hell, no," Faro said. He leaned forward, at the last moment remembering to place his smoldering cigar on the windowsill, and placed his hands against her boot-clad ankles, then raised them, running his fingers up the springy calves and yielding thighs.

The woman's breath came in fast gasps as she plucked at her traveling coat, unfastening it, then unbuttoned her shirtwaist, baring white, shapely breasts tipped with pale-rose nipples that swelled as he watched.

He withdrew one hand from beneath her long skirt and undid the front of his trousers, letting his erection spring out; her eyes widened in admiration and delight. "Oh, that is going to feel *so* good," she murmured, then giggled as the sleeping Army officer stirred and gave what might have been a strangled snore or a belch.

Faro grasped the hem of her skirt and lifted it, bunching it around her waist, a little surprised but not at all displeased to find that she wore no drawers, and was visibly and bountifully ready for him.

He rose and moved to her; her legs parted and a slim hand reached to guide him into her—

—And the stage's wheel passed over a rock in the trail, giving it a severe jolt, snapping Faro out of his half-waking fantasy.

The woman passenger was still opposite him, dividing her attention between a book she was reading and the passing Badlands landscape; the Army man was still passed out in the corner. Everything was as it had been for the last three hours, which was to say damned dull. No wonder, Faro thought, that a man'd fall to daydreaming; nothing else to do, if you don't have a mind to read. The only reading matter he had with him was the 1878 edition of E. N. Grandine's catalogue of card-sharping and general cheating devices, which he preferred not to study in public. It was a necessity in his trade, but people were all too ready to assume that a gambler who was fully informed on how to cheat without detection *would* cheat; and this was foreign to Faro's principles, except when absolutely necessary.

That had been some daydream, for sure, he reflected, almost as real as if it had been happening. He was thankful that his broad-brimmed hat was resting on his lap, else it would have been all too clear to the woman how his thoughts had been running.

He studied the woman, careful not to glance at her too directly and so perhaps alarm her; unescorted females out here—and elsewhere, for all he knew—were apt to suspect any man looking closely at them of having designs on their virtue and carry on about it, and maybe, most of the time, they were right. She was a fair looker, maybe a touch on the sunny side of thirty, a little too strong in the face to be really pretty, but undoubtedly interesting. The jacket and skirt, both cut sensibly long for travel, could have concealed about what he had imagined; at least, she wasn't obviously pudgy or bony. He wondered if she did in fact wear drawers. Probably; in his daydream he'd been anxious to get to the point and hadn't wanted to bother with the tedious business of sliding them off and working them past her boots, a difficult maneuver which had once or twice in the past brought some diverting proceedings to a halt. The thing to do was get the boots off first, then the drawers could just be kicked away. And then, skirt up and cock out, get at it. . . .

Faro shook himself almost imperceptibly and turned his mind away from the imagined picture. Faro Blake, he told himself silently, you can let your mind wander up them interesting byways until you give yourself a mortal case of the hot rocks, or you can turn it to something that'll do you some good.

Like what's the chances of putting together a stake of ten thousand or so in Deadwood pretty quick?

Ten thousand was what it would take to sit in comfortably on the game Jim McGaha was going to be setting up in St. Louis in about three weeks. And it would be a game and a half, and no mistake, with the neck-or-nothing gentlemen gamblers like his old crony "You

Lose" Lewis, and the professionals like Faro himself drifting in from halfway across the country for it.

Denver, the last big town he'd been in, would have been the logical place to build up his stake. But he had had the misfortune to win an argument over an extra ace that had fluttered to the floor from an opponent's sleeve by being a shade faster with his Reid's .38 "My Friend" knuckleduster-pistol than the cheater had been with his vest-pocket derringer. Since the man had been observed in the act by a crowd of witnesses, and was a known pimp to boot, Faro had not expected any problems over the matter. However, the loser in the dispute had been the fancy man of one of Denver's best-connected prostitutes—connected several times a night, as it turned out, to judges, police officials, bankers—just about every influential male the town boasted. The only consolation the lady wanted, and without which she threatened to withhold her favors indefinitely, or at least raise her prices to a prohibitive level, was Faro Blake's head.

The Denver elders were not ready to take such a drastic step, but they didn't choose to be cut off from their favorite recreation; and a satisfactory compromise was reached by booting Faro out of town with orders not to return unless he had posted a deposit with the local undertaker sufficient to see to a decent burial. This formula at least satisfied the bereft lady and her patrons. Faro thought it stank.

By this time, any of the major centers he could have got to quickly would be aswarm with gamblers doing just what he meant to do, playing hard and cutting corners to get together the cash that would be a passport to Jim McGaha's game.

What he needed was a place where there was money to be won and a population ready to give him a chance of winning it—but unattractive enough so that there wouldn't be too much competition. Deadwood in the Dakotas seemed to fill the bill on all counts.

The boom of the first Black Hills gold strike a few years back had subsided, but there was plenty of high-grade ore still being dug. The motley population of miners, prospectors, trappers, hardcases quartered in the Missouri Breaks and occasional Indians drifting in had few pleasures but drinking and gambling; so the first two requirements Faro was looking for were easily met. And as for the third, Deadwood was regarded in the gambling fraternity as a good place to stay away from; Wild Bill Hickok, backshot there in '76, hadn't been the first or last gambler to play his last card in Deadwood. Faro would have an almost clear field, as long as he survived to use it.

The sound of the coach wheels and the hoofbeats of the team drawing it took on an echoing quality, and the sunlight angling in from the right-side windows was cut off. Faro glanced out and saw that the coach had entered a narrow draw, a cut in the distorted red-streaked rock that formed most of the landscape.

The woman opposite him laid down her book and looked uneasily at the rockwall flashing by them and the brush-grown lodge that topped it, perhaps ten feet above them. Faro, as he had many times since the woman had boarded the coach—and the Army officer, a captain, had been pretty much poured onto it by a sour-faced sergeant—wondered what she was. The most likely guess was that she was somebody's wife, maybe an Army man's or a rancher's, traveling to join him; but she didn't, somehow, have a wife-look. There was an air of competence and independence about her that suggested that she wasn't accustomed to depending on some man for her living and function. A schoolmarm? Maybe, but her clothing and the traveling bag on the rack overhead were, though now somewhat dust-stained, better quality than a teacher's wages would run to. Maybe something high-class in the way of whores? A little cold-looking for that, and, anyhow, Deadwood would be an unlikely destination for anyone in that line who wasn't about played out.

The woman darted a glance ahead and upward—Faro, riding in the backward-facing seat, could only see what was alongside and beside the coach, not what lay in front of it—and plunged a hand into the capacious purse which lay on her lap.

At the same time as she withdrew a nickel-plated revolver, the team's hoofbeats quickened and the coach sped ahead; from the driver's seat above there came a hoarse cry and the crash of a shotgun; and Faro saw a near-naked figure with a painted face leaping from the ledge for the side of the coach.

The woman fired twice, and the attacking Indian crumpled in mid-leap; but two others were scrambling down to the track, disappearing from view as they came close to the coach.

Faro drew the Reid's, bitterly regretting the absence of the cut-down shotgun packed in his valise on top of the coach. With barrels and stock drastically truncated, it was little larger than an old-fashioned dragoon's pistol, but was a powerful argument in any close-range contentions. When he was anticipating trouble, it was his custom to wear it in a specially designed sling which concealed it under his frock coat; but the worst he had expected from this leg of the trip was dust and boredom.

A hand and arm snaked through the window and snatched the pistol from the woman's grasp; then the window frame was half-filled with a glaring, painted face, a sweat-streaked torso and the same hand and arm bringing the shiny pistol to bear inside the coach. Faro jabbed the Reid's against the Indian's chest and pulled the trigger as rapidly as he could.

The attacker flew backward as if struck by a twelve-pound sledge, and the nickel-plated pistol clattered to the floor.

The woman snatched it up and peered out the window of the coach, which was now rocking dangerously as it sped along. Faro jammed himself into the opening alongside her and looked back along the coach track. They were in the open now, and at the end of the draw, he could see two sprawled figures, and another scrambling up to where three ponies stood patiently.

"He could catch up with us," the woman said, "but there'd be no sense to it. Out in the open, either of us or the driver could pick him off before he got close. Now that the ambush has failed, he'll give up. For now, anyhow."

Faro was vividly aware of the woman's bodily warmth through the layers of her clothing, and the soft feel of her arm and flank against his. He was, he realized, suddenly and fully erect. Now that he thought about it, he supposed he must have been terrified during the attack, but had been too busy to notice; now, reacting from that, he had a powerful wish to fuck his brains out.

The woman glanced at him, then slid away and resumed her seat. He wondered if she had felt the same impulse. If so, the moment passed as the coach slowed and stopped and the driver jumped down and peered in.

"You folks okay?"

"Right as rain," Faro assured him.

"Jesus!" the driver said, looking past the woman. "They got the captain, though."

"No," the woman said, glancing at the limp, slack-jawed officer. "He slept through it. None the worse for wear, more's the pity."

When the coach resumed its journey, Faro felt that the recent events justified a little informality—if you've joined a woman in fighting off an ambush, an introduction isn't strictly necessary.

"What was all that about, d'you suppose?" he asked. "I mean, your normal stage robbery is a kind of business proposition, with the fellows out after something valuable, and the killings, if any, being done only if there is some kind of commercial necessity to them. But that crowd seemed mainly to want us dead."

"Not so much us as him," the woman said, nodding toward the sleeping officer. "That's Meyner, the one they call the Butcher of Crow Creek."

Faro recalled having heard something about the Crow Creek massacre some months back—a cavalry raid on a peaceful Indian settlement, wiping it out to the last man, woman and child. The gossip had it that the officer in charge—yes, name of Meyner, he recalled now—had been drunk, lost contact with the war party he was pursuing and had decided to have some Indian casualties to show for his effort.

"I can see that they would hate him like poison," Faro said, "but it seems a little like going overboard to drag us into the fight—you nor me nor the driver didn't have nothing to do with Crow Creek, not even being in the Army."

The woman looked at him sharply. "They don't see it that way. To their way of thinking, the whites don't belong out here, and it's only people like Meyner who make it possible for them to settle and travel—so any white, even one that hasn't personally done them harm, gets the benefit from those that have, and they don't worry overmuch about getting a few so-called innocents if they're after a real enemy."

She studied him intently. "I don't know that I've met anybody out here who's quite as detached as you about this whole question. Everybody's either all the way against the Indians, and'd like to see them all wiped out so that the whole West could be turned into a kind of Ohio, with farms and ranches and towns and banks all over the place; or they've got some remnant of decency left, and want the Indians to be treated justly and with respect."

"Well," Faro said, "I am not in the pioneering business or the settling business or the Indianing business, so I figure it ain't my concern. I would like to get on with my trade without all them complications, and leave them to those that has a stake in them."

The woman looked at him again, expressionless this time. It was as though her eyes were the lenses of a stereoscopic camera, registering the details of his appearance—the black frock coat and trousers, linen shirt and string tie, wide-brimmed hat, the greenish eyes, high cheekbones and sandy hair and moustache that gave a hint of the cougar to his face—and focusing them on some glass plate within her mind, where, after a while, they would develop into a picture she would retain with total clarity as long as she chose to.

"A gambler, right?" she said after a moment. "Your outfit, your attitude. . . . I'd say they'd have to add up to that."

"And you'd be right," Faro said uneasily. "Ah . . . you wouldn't happen to be with the Pinkertons, would you, ma'am?" He hadn't actually heard of woman detectives, but, what with Victoria Woodhull running for President six years ago, and women voting in Wyoming, anything could happen.

"No, I'm a journalist," the woman said. "Melissa Chapman, Mr. . . ?"

"Blake," Faro said. "Faro Blake, named for the game, not them old-timey kings in Egypt."

"Then I was right about your work, evidently. That's good; it's part of *my* work to size people up and be right about them most of the time. I write for *Copley's Weekly,* of which you may have heard."

"That the one with all the steel engravings on every page?" Faro asked. "A wonder to me how they get all them lines etched and printed up each week, everything shaded and drawed so natural, you could mistake it for a tintype."

Melissa Chapman gave him a frosty look. "You're probably thinking of *Harper's,* or possibly *Leslie's. Copley's Weekly* is intended for an audience which has not forgotten how to read and doesn't depend on *pictures* to understand what's going on."

Tsai Wang in San Francisco had once told Faro that one picture was worth a thousand words, but he didn't suppose that someone who made her living out of words would see it that way.

"You out here to do a piece on pioneer women braving the perils of the prairie to make a new life, bringing culture and civilization and church socials to the rude frontier?" Faro asked, vaguely recalling pieces by lady journalists he had come across. "Or soiled doves that has redeemed themselves by turning out to be angels of mercy in times of disaster?"

Melissa Chapman threw him a look of exasperation and contempt. "Lord give me strength! You have just seen me fire the first shots in an Indian attack and likely kill a fellow human that was trying to kill *me,* and not need any smelling salts to keep me from going into *womanly* hysterics, and yet it doesn't occur to you that I could write about anything but *women's* stuff! If you want to know, Mr. Blake, I am working on a series of articles about the terrible deal the Indians out here are getting—*and* just who is getting rich out of it. Well, Mr. Blake, maybe that *is* women's writing, come to think of it. For sure, I don't see any men paying attention! So I write what I damned well please, and what I think needs to be written. And if that's lady-journalism, it's all right with me!"

"No offense meant, ma'am," Faro said.

"That's the worst of it," Melissa Chapman said gloomily. "You just take it for granted that a woman's not to be taken seriously. I will tell you, I am putting together a story that will be the biggest scandal since the Crédit Mobilier, and the chances are it'll be laughed off because I'm female. Whatever I'm lacking because I'm not a man, it isn't brains, an eye for what's going on and a hand to write it down. I am out here, Mr. Faro Blake, to write the story of how the Indians are being systematically exterminated, and write that story in such a way that public opinion will force the Government to reverse their policy and curb the murderers like Captain Meyner here."

"For someone who is pulling for the Indians, you were pretty quick at loosing off at that first visitor we had," Faro observed. "If you didn't exterminate him outright, I'd hazard that you switched him over onto that track pretty decisive."

"I am here to write dispatches that will help the Indian people as a whole," Melissa Chapman said. "I can't afford to let some misguided soul spoil that by killing me, can I?"

"Maybe a shame you didn't let him have a try at the officer and gentleman over there," Faro said. "One murderer the less, the way you tell it."

She shrugged. "Meyner's a brute and a fanatic, but he's not really important. There are always people like that. The real problem is the Federal Government and its policies. They look good on paper, full of noble ideals and helping our wild brothers and so on, treating them with full generosity. Only the trouble is that that generosity is dealt out by the Indian agents the Government appoints, and an awful lot of them are outright scoundrels. They collect money to provide the reservation Indians with food and supplies, and then deliver— when they deliver anything at all—scrawny, worthless cattle, rotten meat, weevily grain and worn-out blankets and clothing. There's evidence that up to three-quarters of what some agents are getting from the Government for the Indians sticks to their fingers. The Indians don't mind too much about the agents swindling the Government—that's the way whites behave, as far as their experience shows—but when they're cramped onto reservations, forbidden to use their hunting grounds and left to starve, freeze and die of sickness, why, then some of them start breaking out—and then the Meyners and the Army people who support them get turned loose."

"And I would guess it ain't no use them complaining to the Government," Faro said, "as, with that kind of money into it, nobody'd get the agent job without some pretty good friends in Washington."

"Precisely," Melissa Chapman said. "But I hope that my articles will raise enough of a scandal so that something'll be done. If they sell enough copies of *Copley's,* the other magazines and papers'll jump onto the topic, same as happened with the Crédit Mobilier—and that wound up, you may remember if you ever look up from the card table to see what's going on, in shaking a lot of rotten apples loose, and nearly brought down the vice-president. And, after all, there is another side to the story. You can't say that everyone in government's for sale, and there really are some good and concerned men involved in Indian affairs. There's a man named Buckthorn I want to talk to in Deadwood, that's why I'm going there. He wants to be appointed Indian agent for the region and, for a wonder, he's come out to study what the problems are and what the job calls for. As far as I can tell, he's something new in this sorry business, a man with ideals. And he's well-enough off not to be in it for the money, plus being well-connected in Washington. Educated at Columbia, intelligent, honest—if a man like that can get appointed Indian agent here, it could mean a whole new era for the Indians. And if what I hear about him is true, I'll be proud to see that *Copley's* does what it can to see that he gets his chance."

"Seems a lot to put on one man," Faro said, recalling a number of boom towns that had thought that importing a famed lawman would clean up their criminal problems, then found that the Millennium was no closer, and maybe a touch more distant.

"It's a start, anyhow," Melissa Chapman said. "At the least, he'll have some influence in Washington, and could see to it that Meyner and his like don't have it all their way. The wind's changing a little in the Army, too, which is a good sign. The inquiry after Crow Creek exonerated Meyner—but it's known that he's been passed over for promotion once already, and he'll never get any higher than captain. So even there, there's something to work with, some signs of conscience."

Faro nodded, but privately considered that there might be a better reason for continuing the Butcher of Crow Creek in grade. The Army was stuffy, and "Major Meyner" would sound just too damned silly.

CHAPTER 2

"I'll call the last turn," the tall man in the gray suit said, his nasally twanging accent turning it into "Al cawl the laast tuun." He towered over the green felt faro layout in the back of the Star Saloon, reminding Faro strongly of a stork, with his hunched shoulders, beaky nose and air of concentration.

"The ace, the seven and the hock card's the trey," the man went on.

Faro slid the top card of the last three remaining in the deck out of the dealing box: ace of hearts. Then, as the tall man had bet, the seven of diamonds and the three of hearts.

As called for on a last-turn bet, Faro paid out four times the tall man's stake. This was less of a blow than it might have been, as the stake was—as it had been for him throughout the hand's twenty-five turns—one dollar.

"Excellent," the tall man said, raking in his winnings.

Faro raised his eyebrows. By his reckoning the man had about broken even, which was better than most of the other players had done, but still no cause for self-congratulation.

"Twenty-five dollars wagered, twenty-four won, for a net loss of one dollar," the man went on, "or four per cent. In these units, that is as close as you can get to the percentage favoring the dealer, which is between two and three. It is always satisfactory to see the laws of chance working out precisely."

A large, ruddy-faced young man, who had taken his losses of just over a hundred dollars genially, laughed and said, "Professor, I take my hat off to you. Only a Harvard man could approach gambling so bloodlessly."

The professor peered at him and said dryly, "Mr. Buckthorn, it's to be expected that a graduate of one of our newer institutions of higher learning—your charter goes back no further than 1755, I believe—should value recklessness rather than the contemplation of the marvelous precision of the laws of nature and the mysteries of the mathematical structure that underlies them."

Buckthorn chuckled. "I'd say you'll want some recklessness out on your diggings, sir. What with Indians, outlaws and weather, it'll take more than contemplation to get those old bones out of the ground. It'd be a lark to come give you a hand, and I'd do it if I weren't so confoundedly busy here."

For all the refinement of language, the two reminded Faro of two trail hands amiably hoorawing each other. An education, it struck him, was something that let you do just the same things as anyone else, only with more polish.

A short man in greasy buckskins, whose bristly hair and whiskers gave him something of the appearance of a beaver that had started to shave and then thought better of it—a winner to the tune of about thirty dollars—spoke up, tugging at the professor's sleeve. "You digging up them old stone bones the Injuns talk of, Perfesser? That your line of work?"

"It is, sir," the professor said. "I'm Salathiel Fenn, Professor of Paleontology at Harvard University, and my line of work, as you call it, is therefore the study of fossil remains."

"True what they say, that them's critters that was drownded in the Flood?" the whiskery man asked.

Faro shuffled the cards and slid them back into the dealing box. He debated whether to deal another game right now, or break for a belated supper of a sandwich and a drink. It had been a long day, what with the stage ride and the Indian attack, and, while it had been a good idea to get set up and in business right away, he felt he could use some time off. In any case, right now the prospective players seemed more interested in talking than in gambling. He neatly folded the two-by-three-foot green felt cloth of the layout with each card of the spade suit painted down the center and placed the square abacus-like case-keeper on top of it.

"No, sir, it is not true," Fenn said. "That there was a flood as described in Genesis is a matter of debate, though there is recent evidence of such an inundation—"

"Debate!" The whiskers quivered with shock and indignation. "Why, man, it's wrote! In the Book!"

"—but the fossils with which I am concerned far antedate any such event, I assure you. They are of the Jurassic period, and may be roughly considered to have originated some one hundred fifty million years ago."

The whiskery man gaped. "Now, that is so far wrong it ain't even worth callin' a lie! There is scholars that has worked it out from the Book, by countin' up the begats an' such, that the world was created less 'n six thousand years back!"

"October of 4004 B.C.," Buckthorn said with a grin at Fenn.

"Thass it! This gentleman knows the truth of it!" the whiskery man said excitedly.

"I am aware of Archbishop Ussher's chronology," Fenn said. "But I will tell you that it has nothing to do with science, sir. When we establish that it takes so many thousands of years to lay down an inch of sediment and compress it to rock, and we find hundreds of feet of such layers, it is a difficult but certain process to establish the age of remains found in any such layer. And anyone who can count will come up with the same result—a matter of hundreds of millions of years."

His opponent spluttered with rage. "Thass as much to say that Scripture lies, man! I sooner b'lieve a Yankee perfesser'd lie or is wanderin' in his wits than go against the Bible!" He glared, clenched his fists, and seemed ready to launch himself against the gangling Fenn.

Faro sighed and slid a hand under his coat to reach for the Reid's tucked into his vest pocket. A brawl would complicate his standing with the saloon's management, and if it looked like coming to that, a smart rap behind the short man's ear with the knuckleduster end of the pistol would be called for. He wondered how much force would be required to compensate for the mat of hair.

Buckthorn stepped forward and laid a hand on the short man's shoulder. "Now, gentlemen," he said, "I don't see any need to quarrel over this."

"The quarrel's not of my seeking," Fenn said stiffly.

"A blasphemer's a livin' quarrel with any righteous man!"

Buckthorn patted the tensed shoulder soothingly. "Now, just think about this," he said. "The Bible says that the world was created in seven days, right?" At the short man's nod, he went on, "But it doesn't say anything about what was created *inside* it, does it?"

Faro looked at Buckthorn with interest; Fenn, with some disgust.

"I mean," Buckthorn said, "Adam was created out of earth, and Eve out of a rib—but there's lots more than dirt inside us, blood, bone, guts. And the Bible doesn't go into any anatomy lessons, does it? So, it could be that it's the same way with the earth—it was created with a whole sort of storybook right inside it, those old bones and layers of stone and so on. It wouldn't have been much of a Creation, would it, if the Lord had just slapped together a ball of mud? The way it is, there's lifetimes of wonders for long-headed fellows like Professor Fenn and Professor Handel—" he flashed another grin at Fenn as the professor glared in response to the introduction of this new name "—to practice their learning on. Couldn't that have been the way of it, Professor?"

"I'll allow that it's a proposition impossible to argue against with any logic or rationality," Fenn said coldly.

The whiskery man relaxed. "I'm glad to see you're man enough to own yourself in the wrong," he said. "Makes my blood boil to hear a man denyin' Scripture, so it does." He glanced at the clock over the bar. "I better be gettin' on over to the factor's office. I traded some dumb Injuns out of a load of prime pelts fer some muskets that the locks is rusted shut on, and I want to see how much I made on the deal. So long, gents. Perfesser, I'd recommend you read your Bible some; it'll make a better man of you."

Joined by Buckthorn and Fenn at the bar for his late-evening meal, Faro listened with interest to their conversation. The Professor Handel, the mention of whose name had so irritated Fenn, was, he gathered, a rival paleontologist, a German from the University of Göttingen. According to Fenn, he was an incompetent scientist and an unprincipled scoundrel. As far as Faro could see, the incompetence consisted of disagreeing with Fenn, and the rascality of having beaten Fenn to a prime digging area nearby.

"I've had word that he's uncovering an allosaurus skull in fine condition," Fenn said gloomily. "If he finds the rest of the skeleton, it'll be a considerable coup for the damn Dutchman, no question about it."

Faro asked what an allosaurus was; it turned out to be a big lizard, something like a kangaroo only maybe six times the size, with teeth close to a foot long, that had made its living by killing and eating anything that came near, or that it could catch. The other creatures Fenn and Handel were after were no more appetizing: monsters that had hopped, lumbered or crawled across the ground or flapped through the sky. It was Faro's opinion that they had best be left where they were, instead of wasting time and money digging them up.

"Admired the way you got that sawed-off fellow to simmer down," he said to Buckthorn.

Fenn snorted. "Casuistry! Pandering to ignorance and dogmatism!"

Buckthorn grinned. "Diplomacy, Professor," he said. "Though I'll allow that it often works out to the same thing." He frowned. "But I don't know that I wouldn't have let it come to a fight, then given myself the pleasure of dealing him a few clouts, if I'd known about his swindling those Indians. That's the sort of thing that's poisoning this whole frontier."

"Understand you got ambitions to see that things run different," Faro observed.

"How do you come to understand that?" Buckthorn asked.

"Come in on the stage with a lady writer from some

Eastern weekly," Faro said. "Name of Chapman. Means to look you up and give a boost for you getting the Indian agent job, she said."

"Oh, Lord," Buckthorn muttered. "Some notional old biddy that's an aunt or a cousin to the publisher and got sent out here to keep her out of his hair, I don't doubt. When she gets done with me, I'll probably look so foolish in print that it'll make getting the appointment twice as hard."

"Not my impression of her," Faro said. "Seemed to have her head screwed on straight." He did not volunteer that Melissa Chapman was outstandingly attractive and a cool-nerved and deadly shot. Buckthorn seemed pretty sure of himself, and it would be interesting to see what happened when he came up against something that wasn't quite what he'd expected.

Back at his rear table, Faro soon attracted a small knot of players anxious to buck the tiger. Fenn and Buckthorn were not among them. The professor declared himself ready to turn in early in preparation for his return, the next afternoon, to the digging site in the Badlands. "I could have started out today," he said, "as I've got all the supplies I need bought and loaded, but I calculated that I could use a night of civilized diversion and a little indulgence in the fleshpots, so to speak. With my crew, I can't keep liquor in camp, else they'd sniff it out and get roaring drunk, lose God knows how many days' work."

Buckthorn confessed to a desire to sit in on a poker game or so, which could be satisfied at the Yellowstone down the street. "Faro's a nice pastime," he said, "but it's not in it with poker for interest—you can't try to bluff the dealing box."

"I'll be dealing poker another time, maybe tomorrow," Faro said.

"Be glad to come up against you," Buckthorn said, and nodded a good-night to him.

Most of the new set of players were small-timers, placing minimum bets and coppering close to half of them, laboring under the delusion that this was somehow a conservative policy. The one big bettor was a casually dressed man of about forty, perhaps six or so years Faro's senior, whom Faro found it hard to classify. He could have been one of the rule-bending lawman of the Masterson stripe or an outlaw or a rancher —even, though his style of play didn't indicate it, a gambler. Whatever he was, Faro decided, he was a tough nut, even though he had an outward air of relaxation.

"This is my lucky game," he declared at the outset of play. "Played a couple of times at the Suicide Table in Virginia City—both times, me and the other fellows cleaned out the dealer so bad he kilt himself."

"This ain't no suicide table," Faro said sourly. He recalled the story all too well. One Black Jake, dealing from the table in the Delta Saloon, had lost $70,000 in one night, shortly afterward deciding that a bullet was preferable to poverty. The next owner's first night at the table had been his last; he lost far more than he could pay, and forestalled his creditors by following Jake's example. As Faro recalled, the table was now stored away, since nobody cared to risk using it.

"Any faro table can be a suicide table, things go right," the man said cheerfully. "C'mon and git the soda card out of the way, and I've got ten dollars says the seven's the first winner."

"Plain limit's five, like I said at first," Faro advised him.

The man shrugged and pulled back five cartwheels from the seven of spades painted on the layout. "Okay, s'long's there's no shit about a runnin' limit, and I c'n parlee all the way."

Faro considered briefly. The running limit—meaning that any bet could be no more than four times the initial stake—would restrict his possible winnings on any turn to twenty dollars from this one player. It would also restrict his possible loss to that amount. In a game with a number of players going to the maximum of the plain and running limits, that was the way to come out ahead. But there was only the one big fish this time, and a lot of small fry. To get up the ten thousand he wanted at all quickly, he'd have to allow the man to parlee— double his bets indefinitely—and count on the percentages to make him come out ahead.

After the first ten turns, the man—down close to five hundred dollars by then, having parleed successive wins up to that amount before losing—demanded that the plain limit be lifted. "Nobody else in this game worth spit but me," he argued, "and them's my conditions for goin' on."

"Up to ten, you want it that way," Faro said, and slid the next losing card out of the box, exposing the winner. The man said "Haw!" in delight, and slid his stake and his winnings to another card on the layout.

"Want to call the last turn?" Faro asked a few minutes later.

The man glowered. "Yeah, dammit! The, uh . . ." He glanced at the brass-bound wooden case-keeper, whose sliding beads kept track of the cards played so far, and Faro realized with amusement that the damned fool hadn't even kept track for himself. ". . . ace, six, queen."

The queen, ace and six, appearing in that order, lost the man the heap of gold and silver coins piled on the layout. If he'd won the call, Faro calculated, both of them would have broken about even on the game; as it was, he estimated that he himself was about $2,500 ahead—a full quarter of the stake he'd set as his goal, and on the first night of play in Deadwood. Not bad.

He was a little surprised to notice, now, that the other players had dropped out and drifted away. He would have expected them, even after their own participation had stopped, to hang around for the outcome of the contest between himself and the heavy player.

"Looks like this ain't a suicide table, after all," he observed to the loser.

The man glared at him, then turned away. "Wouldn't be too sure of that," he said, and walked away.

"An angry loser?" Faro turned to see Buckthorn standing next to him.

"Indeedy," Faro said. "Man bets like a fool, then gets sore when the upshot is fitting. Fellows like that've got no business gambling. They ain't got the brains nor the character for it, and just go out of their ways to help me make a living. There ought to be a vaccination against gambling for such, like they got for the smallpox."

Buckthorn looked at him closely. "That's an odd thing to say, Blake. What makes your mind run on vaccination?"

He spoke casually, but Faro sensed a sudden tension in him.

"A joke's all," Faro said. "Like with him, see, gambling's a disease, and if there was a way to vaccinate against it. . . . Say, how'd you do at poker?"

Buckthorn seemed to relax. "You're a humorous fellow, Blake, eh? I like that in a man. Pretty well, pretty well; regained what I lost to you and more. There's one man I think won't ever be the same after finding out that I took the last pot with a pair of deuces against his three queens. I raised him 'til he folded, and the last I saw, he was sitting there, just opening and shutting his mouth like a fish. You feel like giving me a game now? I've got an engagement, but nothing important."

"Well, no," Faro said. "I am some tuckered from the day's journeyings and such, and I couldn't give you the competition you deserve tonight. Tomorrow, or any time, I'd be glad to." And so I would, he thought. A man like that, that enjoys the bluffing more than the game, why, that man is meat and drink to the likes of me. I play the cards and he plays me, and with that setup I'd best bring along a satchel to take away the winnings. "I am going along to the Light of the West Hotel, where I have got what passes for a room."

"Oh." Buckthorn fished his watch from his vest and looked at it. "Perhaps I'll keep my engagement after all, then. I've a feeling my luck's running well tonight, but maybe it'll keep. I'll walk you to the hotel—it's in my direction."

But, whatever the urgency of Buckthorn's engagement, it was not enough to counter the appeal of a crap game he observed in progress as they passed by the Yellowstone Saloon. He abandoned Faro, saying, "I've a tingling in my fingers that tells me I can't lose a roll just now, and there's no point in ignoring that, is there?"

Faro made his way alone down the rutted main street of Deadwood, illuminated only by the wash of light from the many still-open saloons and gambling houses; Deadwood didn't run to streetlamps. He found himself wondering about Buckthorn. Most men with an itch to reform things and correct injustices were strait-laced, zealous types, in his experience, and Buckthorn certainly didn't fit that mold. Maybe being rich had something to do with it—enough money in the bank and the pockets, and you can afford to gamble and lose, and even to put in some time and effort working to help out the Indians or whatever strikes your fancy. He recalled having run across officers—most of them Confederate—who had looked on the War that way.

He hefted the weight of his winnings in his jacket pocket, and grinned. Enough fellows like that sore loser and this Buckthorn, and I can be out of Deadwood in no more'n a week, seems like, he told himself. Feel like celebrating some—but best thing's to get some rest.

The dingy lobby of the Light of the West was lit by a single oil lamp, and the night clerk had vanished. To his surprise, the small barroom tucked in a corner of the ground floor was still open, with a woman standing wearily behind the bar.

"Bit late," he said, approaching her.

"Was expecting another . . . customer," she said. "But it don't look like he's coming along. Likely he forgot he said he'd drop by. Anything I can do for you before I close up?"

"Bottle of bourbon," Faro said. "I am feeling pretty good tonight, and it'll take a couple of belts to bring me down enough to get to sleep."

"Glad to hear it," the woman said dispiritedly. He eyed her, noting that in spite of her listless manner she was—as a proper barmaid should be—buxom, blonde and basically amiable-looking. Close to pretty, if not quite, with hair piled in a Psyche knot, and wearing a drawstring blouse that revealed the outlines of an ample bosom. She handed over the corked bottle and took his money, placing it in the cash box.

"Now, it's a shame that I should be feeling on top of the world and you at the bottom of it, as is plain to be seen," Faro said. "Could I buy you a drink before you close up, or maybe slosh some of this into a glass, so as to cheer you some, Miss . . . ?"

"Mehitabel," the barmaid said. "I thank you kindly, but whiskey gives me a rankling in the innards. Port wine is what I take when I feel the need, and right now, I'll tell you, I do feel the . . . need."

There was something of sadness, something of defiance and something of interest in the look she gave him. Faro felt light-headed, both from fatigue and from exhilaration, and felt also a stirring in his groin.

"Miss Mehitabel," he said, "you have got a nice bar here, but it ain't what you would call homelike and cheerful, not this late at night and all deserted. It'd be my privilege to purchase a bottle of your best port wine and take it and thisyer bourbon and you and me upstairs for a little bit of chatting and drinking what we fancy best. My experience, that's a way to get over chagrins and disappointments that works near every time. I am personally Faro Blake, so now we been introduced, and there ain't nothing improper into it."

She gave him a faint smile, looked past him toward the shut front door and the street beyond, then said slowly, "I think that'd do just fine, Mr. Blake."

Mehitabel's mouth was rich and sweet with the taste of the wine, and her body was ripely yielding against his as they embraced, standing, in his room after the first hastily downed glasses.

Her belly slid gently sideways against the erection that was straining to escape from his trousers. Faro plucked her blouse and camisole out of the waistband of her skirt and slid his hands up her side until they circled and supported her breasts.

She moved away from him a little. "Listen," she said, "I been working behind that bar all day and night, and what with the heat and the beer fumes and the cigar smoke, I am smelling about like a goat."

"Nowheres near," Faro protested, reaching for her. "Not that I got that much acquaintance with goats, but . . ."

"I am closer to me than you are," she said, "and I *feel* dirty and smelly, that's the main thing. Lemme wash up a little, huh?"

Faro sighed, nodded and fetched the basin down from the washstand beside the bed, then poured water into it from the capacious pitcher next to it, and tossed her the sponge the hotel had provided.

Mehitabel drew her blouse and camisole over her head, unbuttoned her waistband, dropping her skirt to the floor, peeled her drawers down over her stockings and boots, which she removed last. She stepped carefully into the wide, shallow basin, bent, dipped the sponge in the tepid water and began rinsing her body with it.

"I'll help you with that," Faro said hoarsely. He took the sponge from her and ran it down her back; she arched under its touch, and a stream of water squeezed from it ran down her back, disappearing into the cleft between her buttocks. He slid the sponge around to her belly, barely brushing the top margin of her pubic triangle, then up, pressing it firmly against one breast and then the other. Her damp buttocks were against his groin, grinding in a rotary motion. The water in the basin sloshed over the edge as her feet shifted position. He slid the sponge down to the top of one thigh; she grasped his hand and moved it to between her legs, clenching them and squeezing hand and sponge until the last of the water ran down her legs.

"Cleaned up now?" Faro asked, speaking with difficulty.

"Enough." He lifted her slick body clear of the basin and swung her around as if partnering her in a square dance, then let go; she hit the bed and bounced gently on the taut counterpane, coming to rest with legs apart and her feet dangling just above the floor.

A shirt button skittered on the washstand, then

rolled off as Faro clawed at his shirt. He cursed, fumbling at his trousers; the bulge of his erection made it hard to undo the buttons. Then he was free of his garments and plunging into her.

Mehitabel shuddered and gasped at the first long stroke, and clamped her knees against his sides.

She was soft and rippling under him, a cushion of warmth and moistness, of musky aroma—the bath hadn't been all that effective, but who cared?—and the sweet wine scent. She moved gently, responding to his thrusts and the urgent sliding of his hands over her arms, face, breasts and thighs. It was a fine ride, for sure, and he felt powerful and elated; but he had a brief flash of wondering what Melissa Chapman would be like—livelier, maybe, but nothing like so submissive and comfortable. . . .

Mehitabel gave a little mewing murmur; he saw that her eyes were closed, and had the sudden thought that maybe she was thinking about somebody else, too. . . . Well, fuck it, what was happening now was damned well enough for both of them.

There was the least flutter inside her, and her mouth —but not her eyes—opened; pink stained her upper chest, throat and face. Faro grasped her buttocks in clenched fingers and drove hard and fast, on the edge of coming, then over it, spasming with the familiar mindless rapture.

He lay sprawled across her for a few moments until their ragged breathing had subsided, then stirred and detached himself from her.

"Could you use another of that port wine?" he asked. "I am for a jolt of that bourbon, myself."

They drank, quiet and companionably naked, side by side on the rumpled bed. After a while, Mehitabel sighed and said, "That was nice, and I thank you for it. It was a help when I needed it, I guess. Maybe what

I . . . what was worrying me isn't as bad as I thought. Anyhow, I can think that now, so I guess it's a matter of being easier in my mind. But I better be getting on."

"Could stay stay the night," Faro said.

She shook her head. "It'd be a pleasure, but I don't think I will. There's things I got to study out, still, and I'll have to do that on my own. You'll be around some time, or leaving soon?" She added this last question with a change in tone, as if something had just occurred to her.

"A week, ten days, I'd say," Faro answered.

"Oh." He was a little taken aback to see that she seemed disappointed. "If you was . . . well, no matter. If I see you tomorrow when I'm tending bar, I'd . . . take it kindly if you just talk to me as if you knowed me as the barmaid, nothing else—that all right with you?"

Faro shrugged. "If it's what you want, sure. Anyhow, thanks for . . . thanks."

When she was gone, he poured himself another drink, lit a cigar and lay back, studying the ceiling. Sad ladies make interesting fucking, he reflected, but there's no denying that they got ways that's hard to puzzle out.

Wonder who the hell she was waiting for tonight, and why the dumb sonofabitch didn't show up?

CHAPTER 3

"I thank you, Professor," Faro said around a mouthful of steak and fried egg, the breakfast specialty of the house, a place identified only, but accurately, as Eats, "but your quarrel ain't my quarrel, and my interests don't run to old bones, except my intention of making some myself, as the saying goes."

"Well, do think on it, Blake," Professor Fenn said, brooding over his cup of coffee and slab of toasted dry bread. "I could surely use a man of your background and ingenuity to help me counter the schemes of that dastard Handel. Not only is the man a villain of the deepest dye, but he has obtained the services of a crew of cutthroats and ruffians who would probably stop at nothing—some of them treacherously hired away from me. The pay isn't much, I admit, as university stipends are not generous, but there are, ah, *opportunities*."

"For informing myself on the looks of a lot of monsters I wouldn't care to see, even with no admission charge, in a carnival sideshow?" Faro asked. "Thank you kindly, Professor, but I will pass on that."

"I meant opportunities more in your line," Fenn said. "The crew would go mad at the chance for some real gambling. If you were to accommodate them, I don't doubt that you'd clean them out within a few days after each payday."

Faro looked at him closely. "That could be the way of it," he said. "But how come that strikes you as a good proposition?"

Fenn chewed a piece of his toast and sipped at his coffee mug. "I've got to pay them every two weeks, d'ye see?" he said. "It's the agreement, and they won't have it otherwise if they're to go on working. But every time they get paid, they slip off to the nearest trading post and get drunk and carry on, and days and days of good digging time are wasted until they sober up and come back. I'd fire the lot of them, but I don't have the time to round up a new crew, especially some of the men that know where the best sites are. It came to me that if there was a man in the camp itself who'd take care of their need to gamble right on the spot, why, then they'd have no money left to go off and drink and lose time."

"That is a neat kind of solution to your problem," Faro said after a moment contemplating it and reflecting on academic ethics, "but I myself am out to lay by a considerable stock of money in the next week or so, and it's the plain truth that there's more of it to hand in Deadwood than there is in your camp, so Deadwood's where I propose to dig in for a while."

"Let me know if you change your mind," Fenn said, rising to leave. "My supply wagon is about loaded, and I expect to be leaving early in the afternoon."

After his departure, Faro dug into the remainder of his steak and eggs. As he was mopping up the last puddle of yolk with a slab of bread, he saw Captain Meyner, his somnolent fellow-passenger of the day before, enter Eats' front door. That was no great surprise, as, from what he had been able to learn, there was no real competition in Deadwood for the breakfast trade—unless it was cause for wonder that Meyner took any nourishment except in liquid form. However, Faro's eyebrows rose as he saw Meyner's companion, Simon Buckthorn. Both men made for a table at the far side of the room, not noticing Faro.

He watched the two men take seats and order, then fall to talking earnestly. Faro rose, paid the cash girl for his meal and left, wondering how it was that Buckthorn, the reformer and would-be Indian agent, was hobnobbing with the drunken and murderous military fanatic, instead of getting Melissa Chapman to push him for the job he wanted. Maybe, he thought, Buckthorn was investigating the kind of opposition he'd have to face if the appointment came through.

Out in the street, he turned in the direction of the Light of the West, intending to put in a few hours' practice with a deck of cards to make sure that his skills didn't get rusty. Not that he had any intention of indulging in any fast shuffles or bottom dealing tonight—he had decided to switch to poker for the day's play, hoping to try Buckthorn's mettle, with any luck, to his own considerable profit—but he had found that, the more familiar his fingers were with any fast work that could be pulled, the more likely his eyes were to spot any examples of it others might try.

"Morning," a man lounging against a store hailed him. Faro recognized him as one of the small bettors in last night's final game. He looked at Faro dolefully, as though paying his respects to the central figure at a wake.

"Morning to you," Faro said. "Expect to see you at the Star tonight? I'll be dealing poker, not faro."

The man shook his head. "Not me, mister. It ain't worth it."

"Lost too much last night?" Faro asked.

"Ain't that." The man studied him. "Bein' new here, I guess you don't know what you done, that game."

"I won it, that's what," Faro said.

"Yah, but it's who you won it off of, d'you see?"

"And who was that?"

"Dirty Dave Fowler, thass who."

Faro shrugged. "Not a name knowed to me."

The man gave a quick look up and down the street, and edged closer to Faro. "Dirty Dave Fowler, sober, is the meanest sonofabitch in or around Deadwood. A killer, a man that'll study out all the ways they is to get the fellow he's after, and do it and walk away from it with nothing to prove he done it. Drunk, he is all right, except when the fit takes him to gamble. He wins, that's all right. But he loses, and recalls it when he sobers up next day, why, then there's nothing but murder on his mind, and he don't rest 'til he's done it."

"Seemed pretty mean last night," Faro said. "He sober then?"

"That was his good side you seen," the man answered. "Drunk enough to be halfway human, Dave was."

"Well, hell," Faro said. "If old Dirty feels he got himself a argument with me, he's welcome to come up against me with gun, knife or thumbs in the eyeballs, and I believe he'll get as good as he gives, with some extra damages throwed in to boot. You want to let him know that, you're welcome to. I will be running my game tonight at the Star, and Fowler can be there or not, as he chooses. I'll take his money if he wants to throw it away again, or his life, if he's set on staking that, or anything in between he likes. I am in Deadwood to do business, and I don't propose to let this Fowler hinder me."

The man shook his head. "No point to your setting out the cards tonight, nor any other. See, Dave ain't like your usual type of gunman, else he'd of gone down in a fight or been strung up long since. What Dave does, he studies out the man he's after, sometimes for a day, sometimes for a week or more, maybe a month, then, when everything's to his liking, why, he strikes swift as a rattlesnake, and there you are. Only what with not caring for witnesses, he's been knowed to use methods that corpse everyone within three yards or so of the intended as well. You will understand that a man that Dave's marked out, well, nobody wants to be anywheres near him until the thing's settled. Unhealthy. So I misdoubt that you'll get any play tonight. Dave ain't been seed this morning, which means that he's gone to ground and is studying out how to settle your hash whenas he chooses to. And until the settlement, you ain't going to have much company. Including mine, come to think of it," the doleful man added hastily, moving off some yards.

In his room, Faro glared at the cards laid out on the table. He had hoped to be able to dismiss his informant's warnings as a tall tale, but inquiry among other Deadwood residents bore out the reputation of Dirty Dick Fowler, and indeed embellished it. Everyone he had consulted had made it clear that, however much they might feel the lack, they would do without the pleasure of attending Faro's poker game at the Star. He had half-decided to make an appearance there anyhow, hoping at least to provoke Fowler into an appearance which would settle their differences one way or another, but the owner of the Star firmly ruled this out, barring him from the place.

"Nothing against you, Blake," he said, "but you got to realize all my stock and fixtures is boated up from St. Louis or Omaha, then freighted crost-country from the Missouri, and all that costs the earth. Was Dirty

Dick to make his play in here, I could be out of business for months."

"Maybe I could get word to him to come at me in a open field, so's there wouldn't be no property damage," Faro said acidly. When he saw the saloon owner's face brighten at this suggestion, he left in a contained fury.

His mood was not lightened when the day clerk at the Light of the West told him, with an unconvincing air of apology, that the whole hotel had been suddenly reserved by a convention of barbed-wire salesmen, and that his room would have to be vacated by sunset, preferably sooner.

He had pondered the idea of seeking out Fowler and killing him, but rejected it. First, he wouldn't know where to look; second, the odds on killing Fowler instead of being killed himself were unacceptably long; third, and worst, even if he did, he'd likely be jailed for it, lacking Fowler's talent for dealing with inconvenient witnesses and the law. Face it, he told himself, the man's a murderer and knows the ins and outs of it. That's his trade, like gambling's mine; I can take him on my own ground, and he can take me on his. In any case, don't look like I got the time left here to get into that kind of project.

He sought out Fenn and accepted his offer of employment as strategic advisor and staff economist in charge of subjecting the crew to enforced thrift, if not actual savings.

The professor was delighted and sent Faro back to the hotel to pack before joining the wagon train.

Now, with a savage glance at the cards on the table in his room, he swept them into his valise. He snapped open the fitted case that held his faro layout and equipment, and a selection of Grandine's "advantage tools" —not for general use, but it was plain dumb not to have the best equipment on hand in case it was needed in emergencies—and took out a cloth-wrapped bundle.

He undid the cloth, revealing the cut-down shotgun, and nestled it in the sling sewn to the inside of his frock coat. With this Fowler business going on, it was the least precaution he could take.

His hand slid under his coat to grasp the gunbutt as a knock came at the door. "Yeah?" he called.

"Mr. Blake?" He relaxed as he recognized Mehitabel's voice.

"Come in."

The door opened, and his eyes widened as he saw that she was dressed in a linen traveling coat and carrying a satchel.

"I heard around that you changed your plans and was leaving today," she said.

"I don't know that Deadwood needs a paper, the way news gets spread," Faro said.

"Take me with you?" she said.

"Since I don't allow liquor in the camp, I don't see that I require a barmaid," said Fenn, surprise and indignation thickening his accent almost to incomprehensibility.

"Well, she can cook up a storm," Faro said. He had no idea about Mehitabel's talents in that line, but assumed that, as a woman, she probably had the rudiments. "I will bet that out at that camp, you don't get but boiled beans and bacon and twist bread cooked on a stick over the fire."

"I have laid in some canned stewed tomatoes and a cask of dried fish this trip; otherwise you're not far off," the professor admitted.

"You turn Mehitabel loose on them fixings, and I promise you a meal you and your boys won't never forget," Faro said. "Listen, there's no pay into it, just her keep, and she'll save you more'n that with her thrifty ways around the cook tent."

"You're sure she's not in some trouble with the law?" Fenn said dubiously.

"The law there is around here, it would take a syndicate of Jesse James and Sitting Bull to do anything that'd make it take notice," Faro said. "She wouldn't say, beyond it was a private matter, but it's plain she was scared bad, and needs a way to get out of town without notice being took, as'd happen if she was to buy a place on the stage. Now, Professor, as a civilized man with all them traditions you got, from the Pilgrims on downwards, can you square it with your conscience to let a poor, defenseless woman await a fate too terrible to think about?"

"Or talk about, at any rate," Fenn said dryly.

"And listen," Faro said, "wait 'til that Handel gets wind that you got your own lady cook in camp to set out nourishing hot meals all proper and such; why, I'll bet his nose'll be so far out of joint, he could sneeze into his ear."

"There is that," Fenn said thoughtfully. "Very well; I can't see the harm in it, and you seem set on it; I agree the lady can join us. Now, how do you propose she do so without attracting the attention she seems to fear?"

Faro had worked that out in consultation with Mehitabel, who was still waiting back in his hotel room. "I give her the word, then she'll slip out the back way of the hotel and along behind the buildings. You just get this wagon here shifted over in front of the alley next the provisions store, sort of casual, just about five minutes after I leave you, and leave the cover on it a little loose, and she'll hop right in with no one to see her do it. She'll be out of sight all the way until we're well out of town."

The professor nodded reluctant agreement, and Faro left to return to the Light of the West to send Mehitabel on her way.

"Mr. Blake!" He turned at Melissa Chapman's hail and saw her standing in the shade of the shedroof that ran along in front of the stores.

"Are you prospering in Deadwood?" she asked.

"I done all right for one night," he said. "But I have decided to move on. There is a opportunity for me to educate myself in the wonders of the past, like big old dragons that has got turned to stone some way, and I don't see that I can pass it up."

"You're going out with Professor Fenn?" she asked. *"That* hardly seems like . . . well, I won't ask questions, though it's my trade."

"You getting anywheres with that Buckthorn?" Faro asked. "Seems like a interesting fellow, though I doubt he'd do well in my line of work. Sort of man who'd draw to fill a inside straight, but's got the sand to take his losses."

"That might be a useful insight," Melissa Chapman said. "I'll keep it in mind."

"Well, I got to go collect my traps," Faro said. "Good luck to you, ma'am."

"And to you, Mr. Blake. It's an important part of both our jobs."

Faro touched his hat and left her. Deadwood was a hellhole, all right, but it was a shame to leave it without having seen more of Melissa Chapman. The memory of his daydream of her in the stagecoach yesterday was somehow more exciting than the recollected actuality of Mehitabel, last night.

The trip out to Fenn's Badlands camp was a full day, and he halted the laden wagon near a rare waterhole just about dusk. To Faro's relief, Mehitabel, who had emerged from concealment only after Deadwood had been lost to sight, had put together a meal that was at least edible out of the provisions Fenn had purchased, and the professor was surprisingly complimentary over it.

Over a pot of coffee boiled on the fire, they talked as darkness fell, Mehitabel taking what seemed to Faro a surprising interest in Fenn's accounts of his work, which seemed to be mainly finding jaw-breaking names for creatures that had never been any use to anybody.

Mehitabel was allotted the wagon for her sleeping quarters; Fenn and Faro rolled up in blankets on the hard-packed ground, each of them, at Fenn's suggestion, some distance from the wagon, to allow Mehitabel a measure of privacy.

Faro, pleasantly tired and replete, lay on his back and watched the bright stars, with the coal of his cigar moving among them like a comet. He more or less expected that Mehitabel would slip out and join him; nothing had been said about that, but it seemed the natural course of things.

After half an hour, it had begun to seem less likely; after an hour, he reasoned that she must have been tired out and gone directly to sleep, and proceeded to do the same himself.

In the morning, he was jerked awake by a harsh and unfamiliar sound. After some difficulty, he recognized this as Fenn's voice raised in song as he splashed his face and arms in the waterhole.

Faro unrolled himself from his blanket, fastened up what buttons had come adrift as he slept and stumbled over toward the wagon, where Mehitabel had added greasewood to the coals of last night's fire, and was frying bacon. Fenn's song and the sheepish but proud

grin with which he greeted Faro, and Mehitabel's relaxed, contented look, gave him the explanation for his
fruitless wait in the night watches.

Why not? he thought. You want to be sure of your
welcome in a place, it pays to get on well with the top
man.

CHAPTER 4

The seating arrangements for the morning's drive were different from those of the day before, with Faro now ensconced in shade and comfort on a blanket roll under the wagon's canvas top, while Mehitabel rode next to the professor, who occupied the driver's seat.

Their conversation drifted back to him. Without giving it much attention, he gathered that Professor Doctor Gottfried Handel, D. Sc. from the University of Göttingen, didn't know his phyla from his genera—at this, Mehitabel gave a slight murmur of protest, seeming to feel that she should raise at least a token protest to vulgar talk—and knew no more of vertebrate anatomy than a farmer.

"Less, in fact," Fenn said. "Farmer's got to be able to tell a cow from a horse if he wants to get the milking or the plowing done, and I doubt Handel could cope with that."

"A wonder," Mehitabel said, "that they made him a doctor if he's all that ignorant."

"As to that," Fenn said darkly, "I've heard that some of the Kaiser's government education examiners have, ah, unnatural tastes. I wouldn't put it past Handel to have secured his doctorate by satisfying them. I will say no more on the point."

"Well, nobody could say *you're* turned that way," Mehitabel said in a low tone that was not meant to carry to Faro, but did.

"Ah, thank you, my dear," Fenn muttered. At a more normal level of voice, he resumed, "But his qualifications and nature are not my chief complaints against the man, Miss Mehitabel. No, it is his underhanded and unconscionable methods that gall me. I had the good fortune to receive a confidential report of a vast deposit of dinosaur bones in this region, and made instant preparations to mount an expedition for the purpose of extracting and classifying them. To my outrage, when I arrived, I found Handel and his crew of thugs—some of them men I had myself engaged by wire, or at least made firm offers to—ensconced on one of the choicest sites. He attempted to counter my objections with the specious argument that *he* had received just such a report from another source, and earlier at that. A lame excuse!"

To Faro it seemed a fairly healthy one, but he supposed that professors saw things differently.

He closed his eyes and sought sleep as Fenn droned on about Handel's iniquities; the German appeared to be capable of anything from theft to sabotage and murder to outright publication of false data, and was plotting some or all of these from his base, not twenty miles from Fenn's own.

"Ha!" Fenn said. "Ha, Blake! What d'you make of that?"

Faro surveyed the elongated hunk of stone Fenn held reverently. "Like somebody tried to make a pickaxe out of stone," he said. "Same size and shape, anyhow."

"The tooth of an allosaurus," Fenn said impressively.

"A hundred fifty million years ago, this very tooth ripped the flesh of countless reptiles, feeding its owner's insatiable hunger. Grand to contemplate it, isn't it? Ha!"

"I guess it is pretty special at that," Faro said. Ever since they had arrived at the digging camp, the professor had been possessed with a feverish enthusiasm, either at being back where he felt truly alive or at the discoveries, such as the giant tooth, that his men had made in his absence.

The men had responded with equal enthusiasm, and considerably more surprise, to the arrival of Mehitabel. Faro suspected that she would be hard put to it to confine her services to cooking.

Faro surveyed the camp. It boasted one rude shack and a huddle of tents, with a small corral containing half a dozen horses to one side, and was sprawled across a rocky stretch of reasonably level ground at the foot of a steep rock slope. This was striped in shades of red and brown, and displayed ripples and bumps which the professor had assured him marked fossil beds. Part of the slope had been cut away by the diggers, and more recognizable shapes protruded, including something that looked to Faro like the shinbone of a man about twenty feet tall.

Some of Fenn's enthusiasm leaked from him as he once more regarded the allosaurus tooth. "The lads tell me that this is all they could recover. Rest of the skull's so fragmented it can't be pieced together. That wretch Handel has the best of it so far, but I'm nearer than he is to getting the skeleton, I'll warrant. He's welcome to his damned skull—it's the body structure that gives you the picture of the beast, Blake. And I'll be the first man that puts one together, skull or not!" He brooded for a moment, then added, "If Handel doesn't try any dirty work, that is. I wouldn't put it past him to steal it when I've got it all out of the rock, or if he can't do that, send his ruffians to smash it to powder." He thought again, hefting the stone tooth in his hand. "Wonder what'd be needed to transport the skull across broken land, at night, say . . ."

At dusk, reclining on the hard earth and regretting a little Mehitabel's decision to see how the dried fish worked with stewed tomatoes, Faro addressed the professor. "Your men seem to be falling in with your plans to relieve 'em of their spare cash," he said. "Not that they've got much left, this close to payday, but they'll give me their markers for what they lose. Could work out for some of them that you'll be paying their wages directly to me. I don't care for that way of doing business myself, but it's your notion, and God knows they're willing to fall in with it. I will set up a faro bank tonight in the cook tent, and get at the good work."

"There!" Fenn said agitatedly.

"Where?" Faro asked. "And what?"

Fenn grabbed his arm with one hand and pointed with the other. "On the skyline, top of the slope, see?"

Faro looked in the indicated direction and caught a glimpse of something large vanishing behind a rock. It could have been a big animal of some kind—or a horse and rider.

Fenn insisted that it was the latter. "A scout for that damned Handel. Spying to see what we've found."

Faro squinted at the darkening sky. "What's left of the light, he wouldn't make out enough to learn spit from. Likely a Indian drifting through, if it was a man ahorse at all." He was getting impatient with Fenn's insistence that his rival was without scruples any stronger than those of old allosaurus. Professors, after all, weren't bandits, though Fenn himself seemed to have some of the characteristics.

*   *   *

The night's play over, Faro took a stroll under the blazing stars to walk off the stiffness of the two hours hunched over the faro table and layout and rid himself of the stuffy, cigar-redolent atmosphere of the cook tent, which he had left enriched by several pieces of paper amounting to a good portion of the next wages due the crew. He had broken, or at least bent, his strict rule of running a dead-straight faro game—a rule arrived at so long ago he was no longer clear about its origin, although he adhered to it—by rigging the dealing box to give him a quite unlawful control over the cards. Operating thus, he was able to keep the men's losses to something they could live with—and, he hoped, let him live with. He supposed it might not have been the best idea to draft Mehitabel to serve as casekeeper. Bent over the abacus-like device and keeping track of the fall of the cards—and wearing the drawstring blouse that showed off her salient features at their best—she had roused the players to a pitch of careless enthusiasm that could have beggared them without Faro's intervention in the operation of the rules of chance. She does that tomorrow, he reflected, I'd better ask her to dig out something that's got more of a neck to it.

He turned and surveyed the few lights in the camp behind him and took a draw on his cigar that puffed it to a flare of incandescence. The place was so peaceful, out under the night sky—and so shabby when daylight revealed it—that it was difficult to think of anyone, even the arch-fiend Handel, cherishing evil designs on it.

Faro abruptly reversed this opinion as something whickered almost in his ear and his hat spun from his head, an instant before the snap of a rifle shot came to his ears, then echoed in the draws and canyons nearby.

CHAPTER 5

"Goddlemighty!" Faro said. "I as near as nothing got a shaft bored through my head you could mine my brains out of, and you are wondering was it Handel done it! Professor, I wouldn't know Handel nor any of them that works for him from Adam's off ox. No, I didn't see who shot at me, Professor, nor I didn't ask him to stop and exchange cards neither. I hit out for a rock to hide behind, even threw away the cigar, which I expect is how he got a bead on me."

He and Fenn were seated in the professor's tent—from which Mehitabel, Faro suspected, had made a rapid exit when the camp came to life at the sound of the shot from the dark. The workmen had returned to their tents by now, and all was quiet once more. Faro picked up his hat, which someone had retrieved from the scene of the shooting and handed him. "Shit, would you look at that," he said. "Holes fore and aft, and no way to patch 'em," he groaned. "Had that hat a long time now, and I don't know where's I can replace it for much under ten dollars. Hell, Professor, it could of been Handel, it could of been one of Handel's men, it could of been a sore-losing Indian, it could of been a fellow that mistook me for a coyote, if coyotes smoked cigars. *I* don't know. What I do know is, I want a stiff drink, and then I want to get some sleep."

"I told you, Blake, I don't have liquor in the camp," Fenn said.

"So you did," Faro said sourly. Behind a jumble of Fenn's equipment, he was pretty sure he could make out the neck of a bottle of port—certainly the one he'd bought from (and for) Mehitabel, night before last, that she'd tucked into her satchel before leaving his hotel room yesterday; but there was no point in making a fuss over it. Besides, there was the best part of his own bottle of bourbon left in his valise in the tent that had been assigned to him; better a belt of that in a couple of minutes than a swig of the sickly-sweet wine, anyhow.

Leaving Fenn's tent, he resolved to pay a visit to the trading post the professor had mentioned and stock up against future emergencies and dry nights. Now that he had what amounted to a mortgage on Fenn's crew's earnings, he supposed they would be glad to have his business. They wouldn't be getting much else.

To his surprise, the post had one other customer when he reached it after a ride of little over an hour the next afternoon. He was riding a horse borrowed from the corral with Fenn's distracted permission; a new bone was beginning to emerge as the rocky slope was patiently chipped away, and the professor had no attention to spare for anything else. The trading post, as he approached it, looked like a lump of mud someone had squared off with a knife after it had dried in the sun. Up close, it looked about the same, except that, from the front view, it had a door opening and two horizontal slit windows.

As he pushed through the door, he discovered that

his entrance doubled the place's clientele. A stocky man with close-cropped graying blond hair sat at the one table, looking with resigned dismay at a mug of beer in front of him. Its head consisted of a few patches of pinhead-sized bubbles which covered about half the liquid's straw-colored surface.

Faro moved to the plank counter behind which the trader stood. "Whiskey," he said, "bourbon if you got it."

"I got a bottle with a bourbon label on it," the trader said carefully. "But I got my own still, and I tell you, what's in that bottle ain't what's wrote on it. I could sell you rye, and you'd get a bottle with a elegant picture of what I would take to be barley printed onto it, or some others, for that matter. But what you are sniffing now," he went on to say, "is what you'll get, leave out what's on the label. That is more in the way of stage scenery, so's the customer gets what he thinks he wants, and don't feel that he's missed out on the color of the frontier."

"Gimme just a plain bottle, then, no label onto it," Faro said. "That way, I won't get the name of no good kind of whiskey mixed up with what I will be getting here."

"That is a good idea," the man at the table said. "It will take me a so-long time to forget that what I have here is sold as beer. I fear that the next tankard of Würzburger I drink will be tainted with the memory."

From the man's comment, his guttural accent and the trader's abashed "Aw, Professor," Faro deduced that his fellow-patron must be Fenn's nemesis, Prof. Dr. Gottfried Handel.

"Join you, sir?" he said, bringing his bottle and a dusty glass borrowed from the trader over to the table. At the German's nod, he sat down, cleaned the glass with his handkerchief, uncorked the bottle and poured himself two fingers of the anonymous whiskey.

They exchanged introductions and Handel—like Fenn in this, Faro noted—immediately plunged into an exposition of his work, evidently discounting the possibility that anything Faro might have to say would be of interest. "With you I can speak freely," Handel declared, after having in his own mind made clear to Faro the principles of paleontology. "I know that pig-dog Fenn's men all too well—some of them he stole from me!—and you are not one."

"Fenn?" Faro said.

Professor Salathiel Fenn, ignorantly granted a chair in Handel's specialty by the upstart University of Harvard, was, according to Handel, a figure of superhuman guile and subhuman morality, a man drawn to science only by greed.

"Didn't know there was that much money in the science line," Faro said, "not unless you was to invent the telephone or a new kind of twine binder."

"If there is, Fenn will find it," Handel said gloomily.

Faro suggested that the professor's beer might be improved, and couldn't be harmed, by a slug from the whiskey bottle. Handel sampled the result, and in a moment became more cheerful. "But Fenn will soon meet his Sedan," he said. "I have unearthed a not-to-be-equaled discovery, the first complete skull of an allosaurus!" This, Handel explained, would establish his paleontological reputation forever, casting Fenn into the eternal shade. "Bones he is getting, I have heard," Handel scoffed. "Bones—a complete skeleton, even— bah! That is nothing without the skull. There, in the brain case, in the jaw hinges, in the teeth, there is where the essence of the creature is to be found. The skeleton tells you no more of that than a coach tells you of the man who drives it."

"Instructive talking to you, Professor," Faro said, corking his bottle and taking his leave.

On his return to camp, after a dusty ride made a little more pleasant by some pulls at the bottle, Faro found it nearly deserted. Fenn and the workmen were still busy chipping at the face of the rock slope; only Mehitabel was present, laying out the supplies needed for the evening meal. He was pleased to see that she no longer wore the fearful look she had had when making her plea to accompany him out of Deadwood. Either she finally felt safe, or she had been comforting herself with the port wine; maybe both.

"You want to get away from this place for a while?" he asked her. She agreed, and they took horses from the corral and rode away from camp. At Mehitabel's insistence, Faro brought along a repeating rifle from Fenn's stock of arms. "Made a rule this morning," she said, "after you went off, that no one was to leave camp unarmed. There is no telling what that Handel would pull, he said, so it didn't do not to be prepared."

Faro debated telling her about his encounter with the fiendish Handel, but decided not to. It wasn't clear where her loyalties lay now, and it wouldn't do for Fenn to hear of his hobnobbing with the enemy.

After half an hour they came to a region which, while still strewn with rocks and studded with grotesque, wind-scoured formations, was less arid than the campsite, boasting patches of scrub and even a few gnarled trees.

"Place to rest in the shade some," Faro said, indicating the largest of these.

"So it is," Mehitabel said.

They dismounted, dropped their horses' reins, and settled on the ground, their backs against the tree's rough trunk. Faro laid the rifle on the ground and slid one arm around Mehitabel's shoulders; she relaxed against him.

She was still wearing the blouse that had bemused the work crew at the faro game last night—maybe washed in the morning and sun-dried on a rock in a few hours, as it was crisp and clean—and the scooped opening at the top invited his fingers. She stirred against him as they slid down the upper surface of her breast and stroked her nipple. It stiffened under his touch. She took a deep breath and laid a hand on his thigh, near the knee, then moving up.

"You're hard," she said dreamily, lightly scratching his erection through the cloth of his trousers.

"You too." He flicked a stiffened nipple.

"There. Not here." She drew his free hand down and pressed it onto the bunched fabric between her legs.

"We got too many damn clothes on," Faro said.

In a moment, they did not, and were grappling, then securely joined, on the sun-dried, pungent grass under the tree. Faro felt the sun bite on his back and legs through the sparse shade of the tree; Mehitabel, under him, was like a pool of cool water to him, warm and vital though she was. The sun glared from the bare rocks nearby, giving reflected light almost as strong as the direct rays would have been. He felt no urgency to complete the act, but a desire to prolong its lazy delight.

Dust fountained six feet away, and the flat clap of a rifle shot sounded an instant later. Faro paused in mid-thrust and glared desperately around. The tree that shaded them was too puny to offer shelter, and the nearest rock of any size was over a hundred yards off. There was nowhere to hide. It was fight it out where he was, or nothing.

"What . . . ?" Mehitabel said faintly.

"Stay still," Faro muttered, and grabbed the rifle and worked the cocking lever. He debated withdrawing from her and moving to one side; but, this way, his body offered her some protection, and he was already in the prone position best suited for returning fire.

If this don't work out, I won't be dying with my boots on, he thought, nor nothing else. Be interesting to know how them that finds us'd handle the burial.

Another shot sent a bullet thudding into the tree trunk. Faro caught the wink of the explosion, centered in a patch of greasewood, aimed and fired, then worked the lever and fired again.

At the noise and the impact of the recoil, Mehitabel shuddered and gasped under him, giving a sudden, urgent thrust of her pelvis. Her legs flexed, then scissored around his thighs.

Dirt and rock fragments showered them from the next shot, which struck only inches from Mehitabel's head. Faro now caught a flicker of motion in the greasewood patch, and cocked and fired steadily until the magazine was exhausted; Mehitabel jerked frantically under him and drummed her heels against his thighs. As he fired the last round, a figure rose from the greasewood with a thin scream, then pitched forward to lie unmoving on the rocky ground.

Mehitabel moaned and thrust hard against him, clawing his back and giving him hard, biting kisses. With a wary eye on the still figure of the ambusher, Faro surrendered himself almost all the way to her passion and his own; they came at the same time in an explosion of almost desperate release.

After what seemed like a long time, he rolled away from her. "I better go see who that was," he said. "You wait here."

"I ain't up to anything else just now, I can tell you," she said faintly.

Without bothering to pull clothes on, but carrying the reloaded rifle, Faro padded across the rocky ground to where the ambusher lay. The man was face-down in the dust, his rifle some distance from his outstretched hand. Faro grasped the head, turned it and stared into the open, dust-filmed eyes, then let it drop.

He rose and started to walk back toward the tree, wondering what the hell had brought Dirty Dave Fowler all this way to try to kill him. The man had a reputation for being a maniac about getting those he fancied had crossed him, sure, but this seemed out of the way, even for him. But that had to be it, no other explanation. And Fowler must have been the rider seen at dusk, and the source of last night's shot from the dark. So that was all cleared up. Fenn might at least be relieved, and not have to worry about sniper attacks from Handel.

He looked ahead toward Mehitabel, still sprawled under the tree, and marveled at what they had just experienced. I would of thought, he told himself, that the chance of getting killed would of frightened us both out of any such notions, but all it done was make it more powerful. That was some doings, but I don't know that I'd want to try it again under them same circumstances.

To his surprise, Mehitabel was shocked and alarmed when Faro told her their assailant's identity, and the shadow he had seen in her face the first time they had met, in the bar of the Light of the West, returned.

He wondered if Fowler had been the "customer" she'd been waiting for that midnight, and the man who had made her so desperate to flee Deadwood. If so, her troubles were over.

Mehitabel did not seem to see it that way. She was silent on the return ride to camp, refusing to respond to his questions or attempts at encouragement, and slipped away from him to begin preparations for dinner.

Faro resolved to have the truth out of her after the evening's game. But she did not appear for it. When he went to search for her, he found her tent empty and her belongings gone; one horse was missing from the corral.

CHAPTER 6

It was not until the next morning that Fenn fully accepted the fact of Mehitabel's disappearance. When he did, it was with a mixture of outrage, disappointment and fear.

"Now, look what you got me into, Blake, and don't deny it's all your fault. That woman used us, and she's made off with one of my horses—what d'you expect me to do about that?"

Somewhat mollified by Faro's offer to pay the cost of the missing animal if it did not turn up, Fenn struck another note. "It's a shame she went off just when we were getting used to her. I'll admit, it made a difference having someone around who could cook properly, and it made the men less rough in their ways and work a little better. I'll have to say that I'll miss her services." And not only in the cook tent, Faro said silently.

A thought struck Fenn that made him start visibly. "D'you suppose Handel got to her, Blake? That he's lured her off so he can have her and not me? It's the kind of thing he'd do—low, sneaking and meant to put him one up on me. Or it could have been a plot from the start, couldn't it? Her planted on me, don't you see, and finding out everything about the camp, then going on to report to him. I wouldn't put it past that devil, not for a minute."

Faro's comment that there didn't seem to be all that much to find out about the camp and its workings failed to reassure Fenn. Finally he returned to the main practical problem caused by Mehitabel's departure. "What we'll do for a cook I don't know. We had only two days of her, but I doubt the men'll have the heart to go back to the old way of one of them taking turns each day. Whatever am I going to do about that?"

Faro looked past him, across the rocky, gully-scarred expanse of plain to the south. "Could be, here comes a replacement now." He could see, in the morning heat haze, a horse and rider, and a following pack mule. They were near enough so that he could see that the rider was a woman.

"I am here on assignment from my magazine and with the permission of your trustees, Professor, to report on your epochal paleontological discoveries. And no, I do not cook," Melissa Chapman said, answering the two questions that Fenn had put urgently to her on her arrival at the camp.

Already confused and dismayed to his limits, Fenn accepted Melissa Chapman's presence with surprisingly little grumbling, allowing her free run of the camp for her work, so long as she did not interfere with the digging or handle specimens except in his presence. In fact, after he had thought about it for a while, he welcomed the prospect of a journalistic report. "A little public interest is wonderful for getting support from the trustees," he said, brightening. "Something that gives Harvard a good name, they'll like that, and chances are the purse strings'll loosen a little. I might be able to get a crew out to Wyoming next year, and there's a lot of work still to be done in Kansas. . . ."

Faro showed Melissa Chapman to her tent, recently allotted to Mehitabel, and said, musingly, "Two days ago you was in Deadwood, hot after Buckthorn and the Indian agenting business. Now here you are, thirsting to write up old lizards and them that digs them out of the ground. There was some quick work into that, I'd say."

She gave him a cool smile. "I had a wire from my publisher instructing me to take on this story, along with wired permission from the university authorities. That's how it is in journalism; you go where you're told and when you're told."

Faro didn't doubt that she'd received the telegrams she'd said she had. What he was not at all sure of was what might have occasioned them—such as an urgent wire originating from Deadwood, Dakota Territories, sent by one Melissa Chapman.

"Mr. Blake, I don't hardly see how I c'n stake more'n a dime on this turn. I already got markers with you that takes up my wages for the rest of the season. I'll be doin' some trappin' in the winter, though, an' I could stake a note payable after May first, '79."

Faro surveyed the work crew, none of whom were much more solvent than the man who had just spoken. "I thank you for your enthusiasm," he said, "but I would say that play is at an end for now. I will leave the layout here and you can play amongst yourselves for matches while I take a turn in the fresh air."

"Ain't the stars bright tonight, Miss Chapman?"

"They usually are, out here."

"Millions and millions of 'em, more'n the eye can see nor count. It makes you think."

"At this latitude, there are about twenty thousand stars visible on a clear night. Mr. Blake, your hand is where it should not be."

"Now, Miss Melissa, I thought you might be a little chilly, out here in the night air."

"I am certainly not in need of warmth where your hand is or where it's approaching."

"But don't it feel kind of good?"

"What you will feel in a moment, Mr. Blake, is the sharp pain of a broken finger if you don't remove your hand. If it's the one you use to deal with, that could be a considerable business reverse for you."

"Good of you to drop in on me, Blake. Nice to have an evening chat after the day's work is done. Though I'd have thought you'd have been dealing your faro bank over at the cook tent, or squiring the elegant Miss Chapman."

"Neither of them propositions is going very well tonight," Faro said.

"Well. Ah, you'll be interested in this. I've almost certainly identified it as part of a vertebra of brontosaurus."

"Another of them killing lizards?" Faro asked.

"No. Brontosaurus was much larger, but herbivorous, as the teeth show. He was so large, in fact, that he required two brains, one in the head to run the front part of him, the other at the base of the spine, to take care of the rest."

"Hey," Faro said faintly, settling himself for another session of boredom. All the same, it seemed the best the camp had to offer tonight.

Now ain't that something, Faro thought bitterly as he picked his way through the darkened camp some time later. Two brains for that old lizard, and here's me, that don't hardly seem to have the one, the fix I got myself into. No chance of making anything like the rest of the ten thousand I need for McGaha's big game here; no chance for some easy rolling with Chapman; and a crazy professor that can't talk but about bones. What the fuck am I doing here? And why stay, anyhow?

Heading for the edge of camp and fumbling at his trousers in preparation for relieving the pressure on his bladder, he reasoned it out. The Missouri wasn't too far to the north. Once there, on a horse borrowed or bought from Fenn, he could take a riverboat down to, say, Omaha. There was a state fair coming up there soon, he remembered, and, even though there'd be a fair number of gamblers working it, he ought to be able to run enough games to come close to making his stake. Fairground crowds were usually easy pickings, more the target of the sharps than the serious gambler, and he generally disdained to practice his trade with them. But right now, after Deadwood, Fowler, Fenn and Chapman—and allosaurus and brontosaurus—he felt entitled to easy pickings. He'd do it.

His mind and his bladder both eased, Faro rebuttoned his trousers, and then tensed. He had heard a clink that might have been a spur hitting rock.

He thought for an instant of calling out "Who's there?" and killed the impulse immediately. Nobody in camp wore spurs except when actually mounted; and now he could sense, it seemed to him, the presence of a number of men nearby. Either several of the crew had come out to take a leak at once, one of them taking a notion to put on spurs for the fun of it, or there were intruders. It wasn't hard to tell what the odds on that were.

As best he could make out, the sounds—the shuffle

of a boot on dirt, the vague stir that even the quietest of men make—came from between him and the heart of the camp.

He had to figure that they would make their move soon; he'd best make his first. He felt for the Reid's in his vest and swore silently. He'd considered that the stubby pistol might be an intrusive presence in the embrace he had hoped for with Melissa Chapman, and left it in his tent, not bothering to replace it when that scheme had soured. So whatever was going on here, he was up against it unarmed.

He recalled the terrain near the camp as best he could. There was a gully that angled to the northwest. If he could get into that, he could evade whatever these fellows had in mind, and circle around to alert the camp.

He crouched and moved forward toward where he thought he remembered the gully began. The blaze of stars made him feel exposed, but he realized that he could see nothing of the details of the landscape, just the shape of the earth where it met the sky, and assumed that he would be unseen by the intruders as long as he kept low.

His booted feet sensed a dip in the ground; he put out a hand and felt the lip of the gully. Once into that and moving quietly, he'd be—

Faro stopped. Ahead of him, looming against the skyline, was a standing figure. A sentinel, Faro guessed, posted to prevent just what he was now trying to do. But, still low to the ground, Faro was as yet unseen. He could stay there, go back or . . .

Hunched as low as he could get, he scuttled along the floor of the gully until he was within three feet of the standing man. He tensed his legs, then sprang, grabbing the man around the knees and swinging him over his head like a flail.

The man's head hit the opposite ledge of the gully with a heavy thudding sound, and he went limp; but not before he had uttered the beginning of a startled cry. Faro heard a stirring and a clatter behind him, then whispered, urgent orders and the pound of feet. He went to step over the sprawled body of his victim; a hand clutched his leg and sent him stumbling.

A hand grabbed at him from behind; he kicked back and up, hard, and heard a choked scream, and the hand fell away. A man showed massively against the skyline for an instant, then jumped into the gully ahead of him. Faro caught the glint of a knife held blade upward. He scrabbled dirt from the gully floor, flung a handful straight at the shadowed head, then rushed to grapple with the man, hoping he'd been temporarily blinded.

Another was on him from behind now, as he struggled with the knife-wielder. A whiskered, bad-breathed head was jammed against his; instinctively he brought up his hand, thumb stiffly extended, and probed for the eyeball—blessing briefly the riverboat fights he'd seen as a boy. The head emitted a howl and fell away.

For an instant he was free, but he could see the pack pursuing him. And then the gully was suddenly and disastrously blocked by a massive rock; water could make its way around it, but a man could not.

Above him, a spiky, thick bush with thorned branches as thick as a stout walking stick had established a foothold. He reached up and, careless of the damage the thorns inflicted on his hands, wrenched a branch loose. The first man to come at him screamed and stumbled aside with his hands to his face as Faro lashed him across the eyes. He felt the thorns dig into and rake the chest of the next man to come at him; then a numbing blow to his arm made him drop the club.

Panting and tired, he drove his fist at the nearest face and had the satisfaction of feeling the crunch of bone under his knuckles in the instant before a smashing blow at the side of his head sent him into darkness.

CHAPTER 7

"Don't see why we couldn't of just corpsed him an' left him there."

"Would of drawed attention, which is what we're ordered not to."

"Well, now, I don't expect the way Fowler was goin' t' work it, the both of 'em shot dead t'gether, would of give anybody any reason t' give the matter a second thought, no, *sir*." The tone was scornful.

"Fowler was plumb loco. If he'd done it his way, he'd of had something to answer for, I'll tell you. But it didn't work, now, did it? And he ain't in charge no more, and I am, so we are following orders from here on. Which them orders is to make it look natural and unsuspicionable."

Faro first registered this dialogue; then other senses returned. He became aware that he was slung over the back of a horse moving at a slow walk, that his hands, bound at the wrists, dangled in front of him, that his ankles, on the animal's other side, were bound as well, that his head ached fiercely and that his tongue seemed to be about the size and consistency of a dried bath sponge.

He opened his eyes and saw from the light on the striped rock formations jolting by him that it was just past dawn. He turned his head painfully and saw that his mount was the last of a line of five; the four ahead of him carried men in a variety of clothing, from a shabby town suit to range gear.

The nearest to him was a massive fellow in greasy jeans and a sheepskin vest, who now said, "So we will take him on a ways and dump him where it will look as if he'd wandered off, got sunstrook or so and laid down and died, all tragic and natural."

"He is looking some used up from that fight he give us," another man put in. "That won't look so almighty natural."

The first speaker shrugged meaty shoulders. "Then we drop him off of a cliff, which will do the job quick and neat, and be reason enough for any bruises or what."

Faro considered his situation and what he could do about it. The situation seemed clear enough: he was being taken off to some place where he could be killed and left as the apparent victim of an accident. Minor details, such as why and at whose orders, were not clear, but not of immediate interest, either. The main thing was how to stop the project before it came to its intended end.

He flexed his legs and arms; the bonds seemed unyielding. If he could raise his hands to his mouth, he might be able to gnaw at the knots that secured them, but it was unlikely that his captors would fail to notice that.

He worked his fingers and felt the ring he wore on his right ring finger rub against its neighboring digit. He had put it on last night as a touch of elegance in preparation for his walk with Melissa Chapman, though it normally had a more businesslike function. Apparently a massive piece of silver, it had glued to its upper surface a carefully polished oval of steel, razor-thin. In a tight game, when it might be necessary to win, without too much regard to the ethics of play, the ring could function as a shiner, angled to give the dealer a brief glimpse of the cards' faces as he passed them to the other players. He hadn't used it professionally since his earliest days as a gambler—his skills were developed far beyond the need for such crude devices, and also it was too obvious and well-known—but it amused him to keep it, along with the other "advantage tools" that he never (or hardly ever) put to use.

He worked his left index finger over to the ring and began prying at the affixed steel oval with his fingernail. As he had hoped, it yielded a little under his prying; he levered the nail further under it until it was almost completely loose from the ring. He pinched it between his thumb and forefinger and worked it free. With an effort that felt as if it would dislocate his wrist, he wrenched his left hand up and began sawing at the thongs that bound his wrists.

He could exert hardly any force, but did feel the steel begin to bite into the thongs. About two hours of this, he told himself, and I might cut through one thong, then get on to the others. And after that, I could study out what to do with my feet. . . .

The prospect was not encouraging, but it was better to be doing something about it than just to lie across the horse like the carcass of a freshly killed deer.

"Was thinkin'," the third man from the front of the file said. "How is it to be knowed we done what we set out to do? I mean, if we hadn't of got hold of him, we could of just rode back an' said we did an' got paid off. An' the story we go back with now ain't no different from what it would of been that way, see?"

"You mean there ain't no proof," the heavy man

said. "Well, shit, he ain't carrying no engraved calling cards nor like that, as we found when we went through his duds, so what can you expect?"

"Now the Injuns," the third man said, "when they go back after a fight, they got somethin' to show for it. Scalps, mebbe a ear or so—even a man's parts, sometimes. Was we to do somethin' like that, it'd look as though some Injuns come acrost him an' done their work, an' we'd have our proof."

The heavy man snorted. "Proof of what? Them items could of come off anybody, nothing to say it's Blake's scalp or whatever. Now, maybe *you* can tell who a man was by a look at his whang and balls, but if you can, I don't know as I ought to be riding with you." He was silent for a moment. "But I'll allow, that injun idea ain't the worst in the world, after all. It'd kind of fit in with the rest, see? Now, if we was to carve him up some and leave him pegged out alongside a trail some place, likely he'd be found in a couple weeks, and it'd be a sure thing it'd be laid to the injuns."

Faro had been looking forward with no enthusiasm at all to the prospect of being thrown off a cliff. Now it seemed like a preferable fate—quick, at least. The only way to present a man convincingly as a victim of Indian torture was to torture him, leaving his dead face distorted with pain and terror. He pinched the steel oval tighter and pressed it harder against the thong.

"It'd look better if we left a arrow in him some place," the lead rider offered.

"Which if we had a arrow, we could do that," the massive man said. "But as all we got amongst us is knives and guns and a saddler's needle for mending harness, I guess we'll have to make do with that. If we come acrost a arrow, I promise you we will use it."

The massive man glanced back. "Hey, Blake's wakeful. Why you a-wriggling of your hands like that, Blake?"

"Tied too tight," Faro called, stretching his neck and twisting his head to face the speaker. "Got to keep working 'em so's they don't go dead and drop off."

The massive man shrugged. "Suit yourself, though it don't seem to me it's worth the trouble."

"Well, it's my hands, so I guess I will keep 'em comfortable as I can while I can feel 'em," Faro said. Sweat was running down his inverted face and into his eyes, blurring his vision, but it seemed to him that the thong he had been sawing at was cut about a third of the way through. "And listen," he went on, "it is not only my hands that's a problem—I been hearing what you said about my scalp, ears and general corpus and your intentions for it, and I would admire to know just what the hell is going on and why."

"For your part in the proceedings, you don't need to know that," the heavy man said. "Now, I got a question—where's that gal you come from Deadwood with, that Mehitabel?"

"Run off from the camp night before last," Faro said. "Took one of the horses and lit out."

"That the truth?"

Faro craned his neck to face the man again, and said, "Would I lie to you?"

The man shrugged. "Why not? But I'll ask you again while as we're getting you to look like the injuns had some fun with you, and I expect whatever you say then'll be the truth."

"This could be a good spot fer it," the man in the lead called. "Likely kind of place for a man to get set on by injuns—thisyer narrer kind of draw, with some brush along the rim they c'n lay hid in. Set Blake out here an' it'll be plain as a picture what happened."

Looking back and up, Faro had to agree that the

spot seemed ideally suited to an Indian ambush. Attackers could stay concealed in the brush until their prey had gone on a little, then part the foliage and peer through . . .

As a painted face was doing now.

He thought of calling out to warn his captors, then wondered what good that would do him. The Indian represented a change in his situation, and any change, it seemed to him, had to be for the better.

"Now," the massive man said, "just up ahead is where we'll—shit, mama, mama, mama!"

He toppled from his horse, the feathered shaft of an arrow protruding from the back of his neck. A gobbling scream came from the sides of the draw as an Indian leaped down it and ran for one of the three men still mounted. Faro heard the snap of rifle fire from the brush, and the lead rider rose in his saddle and slumped forward. The horse carrying Faro reared and bolted. Faro had a glimpse of the massive man lying in the trail, with the head of the arrow sticking out the front of his throat, his mouth working soundlessly. Then the panicked horse's right rear hoof took him squarely in the head.

Faro's still-tied hands scrabbled frantically at the horse's hide as the animal reared again and pivoted, nearly slinging him to the rocky ground; then it plunged down the trail in the direction in which it had come, away from the fight.

He twisted his head to look back. The receding scene was blurred with powder smoke, but he could make out some struggling figures, only one still mounted; and, as he watched, that one was jerked from the saddle. To his relief, neither his former captors nor the Indians seemed to be paying any attention to his fleeing horse.

It seemed to him likely that if any of the men who

had captured him survived the fight, they would get a taste of what they had proposed to do with him. He hoped, spitefully, that they would appreciate the real thing. Though it would have been interesting to find out just what had been the point of all this—Fowler's sniping attack, and then snatching him from Fenn's camp.

Faro estimated that they were at least a mile from the scene of the ambush before the horse slowed to an uneasy trot, and he was able to draw something close to a reasonable breath.

"Now, horse," he said soothingly, "just slow her down a little more, and steer yourself over to some bit of nice grass, if there's any such in this place, and maybe I can roll myself off of you onto where it's soft and do something about being hogtied like this."

The horse subsided into a more placid gait, and Faro began for the first time in what had seemed like hours to feel some hope that things might work out fairly well, at least not fatally. He was almost cheerful as he recommenced sawing at the thongs binding his wrists with the steel oval.

The horse shuddered to a sudden stop. Faro glanced ahead and groaned. What could have been a thick coil of rope lay at the side of the trail—if a coil of rope sported a flat head at one end and a string of rattles at the other, and was ornamented with a diamond pattern.

"Hey, horse," Faro said anxiously, "he ain't aiming to do you no injury. That buzzing he is making is just to warn you to keep off of his patch of rock, see, horse? Now, come on, horse, you just ease yourself over a little sideways, and go on looking for that nice soft patch of grass."

It had always been his firm impression that whoever had fixed on the horse as a riding animal had made a grave mistake. They could cover ground fast enough, if with a lot of jolting, but they struck him as having about the brains of a flea—or maybe, he thought now, of the hind end of the brontosaurus old Fenn had talked about—and a tendency to insane behavior that would make a cocaine-taker seem placid by comparison. His present mount bore this out by screaming shrilly, twisting back and forth violently and then standing almost straight up on its hind feet.

Sky and sunbaked rock alternated twice in Faro's glaring vision as he fell; he had a brief, close-up glimpse of the dusty trail, inches from his eyes; and then the whole planet seemed to hit him a definitive blow.

He came to with dust in his mouth and under his eyelids. He clawed at the hard-packed earth, and then realized that his hands were free. His efforts with the steel oval pried from his ring must have weakened the binding thongs enough so that his impact with the ground had burst them.

He blinked, wincing at the grate of the dust on his eyeballs; the pain made tears come, washing the dust out. Then he groaned, sat up, slapped his head to make it stop aching or at least give it a counter-ache to think about, cursed, profaned, blasphemed and swore in a venomous, continuous mutter, and plucked at the knots that still secured his feet.

All the words, images and combinations he knew or could invent had been exhausted by the time his ankles were finally freed.

He rubbed them until some feeling returned, then stood unsteadily up, stretched, and let his muscles savor the unaccustomed sensation of freedom from bondage.

It had been no fun at all to be slung across the horse's back and led to where he was to be tortured and killed. Now he was a *lot* better off . . . miles from nowhere in the Badlands, hatless against the increasingly intense sun, waterless, and with no idea of what direction to head.

The trail on which the horse had dumped him angled from southwest to northeast, as best he could make out from the position of the sun. He chose the southwest direction; at least, for now, the sun would be at one side, not in his eyes. There didn't seem to be any better reason for making the choice.

CHAPTER 8

Wind or water, long ago, had scooped out softer rock from beneath a more durable stratum, leaving a chunk of it resting like a pot lid on top of a pile of cracked dishes. With the sun almost overhead, it cast a patch of shadow, startlingly dark in this region of sunlight glaring from vividly hued rock. Faro stumbled the last few feet into the shade, gasping with relief as the bite of the sun on his unprotected head vanished.

He sank into a huddled heap against the crumbling sandstone, dimly relishing the sudden coolness and the absence of the constant, blinding light.

Even in the shade, the temperature could not have been much less than that of an oven damped down to keep the food warm; but at least he was not being cooked alive, as it seemed to him that he had been for the last hour of doggedly painful walking. Even his raging thirst seemed just a little lessened by the shade.

It must, he figured, be about seven hours since he had awakened to find himself slung across the horse; a bit more than six since the Indian attack, and maybe five, five and a half since he had come to after the horse had thrown him. If he could get this dried-out, tired and light-headed in that short a time, the chances for making it much farther didn't seem good.

He wished desperately that he had some water; that he had a hat to keep the sun from burning into his head; that he had the kind of boots that would make walking less than a torture.

But I will be dipped in shit before I give up on this, he told himself. I cash in my chips now, and they find me all scrooched up and dried to death, why, that's the kind of thing those fellows that took me aimed to have happen. I ain't about to give them the satisfaction, supposing there is any of them left to know about it or enjoy it.

He rested in the shade of the overhanging rock ledge for hours, wondering if he wouldn't have a better chance moving on during the night, when it would at least be cool. But a painful glimpse across the area ahead of him showed that that wouldn't work. The land was distorted, cracked, tumbled; what looked like a path could become a crevasse or a tunnel in only a few yards, or end in a sudden gulf. The sun would dry him out, but without its light to see by, he would almost certainly break his neck in short order. To live, he would have to keep walking; and, to keep walking, he would need daylight, even if it killed him. Maybe moonlight would have been enough, but, as he recalled from his walk with Melissa Chapman the night before, it was the dark of the moon, with no wash of white light to dim the stars.

He stayed in the shelter of the overhanging rock until the sun dipped enough to wipe out the shade and find him. Its bite was less fierce now as it descended in the west, and he felt almost refreshed as he stumbled on his way.

It seemed less of an effort to walk than it had earlier.

At times he was scarcely conscious that he was placing one foot in front of another.

Ahead of him a bulbous rock formation erected itself against the hard blue sky. As he looked at it, it lost something of its solidity, and seemed to take on vertical stripes. Then . . . of course, that was it, it wasn't a rock formation but a chuckaluck cage. He looked at it closely and, sure enough, it began to rotate. It ejected two dice. Faro looked at where they lay, resting almost against his foot, and saw that they were snake-eyes, a pair of singles.

Don't need that to tell me I'm playing a losing hand, he said to himself, and gave the dice—somehow now about three feet square—a derisory kick as he passed them by.

A little further on—he wasn't sure how much, but the sun seemed lower in the sky—he came to a scatter of giant playing cards set on end, and threaded his way through them. It seemed logical that the first one he came to was the Queen of Spades, the death card. He thumped it with his fist as he squeezed by, and it had the feel of rock. He blinked, and saw it was rock, that he was in the midst of a group of upended sandstone slabs.

It struck him as amusing that his mind was giving out while his feet seemed capable of carrying on without all that much trouble.

"Makes sense," Doc Prentiss said. Faro peered at him, wondering where the old confidence man had come from. Last time he'd seen Doc was over in Texas, close to a year ago. "Situation you're in now, my boy," Doc went on, "sensible thing to do is lie down in a shady spot and die. Got to be crazy to keep on walking in the sun, going nowhere, so the only way you can do it is *go* crazy. Then you don't feel the heat, the pain, the thirst."

Faro grinned. Doc had always been about the best at explaining things of anybody he'd run across. Doc's explanations might not be strictly true, as was to be expected of somebody in the swindling line, but they were always convincing.

He turned to talk to Doc, but the old man was gone, and Nell Garvin was walking beside him, and jaybird-naked at that.

"Hey, Nell," he said, "you'll get sunstruck, no clothes on and all."

"I can take care of myself, don't you worry about that," Nell said. True enough, Faro thought; you don't get to be a successful madam in your twenties without having a lot of what it took to survive. Every time he'd run across Nell, she somehow seemed to come out ahead on the deal. As he looked again at her foxy face and ice-blue eyes, she shimmered and vanished.

Nice of her and Doc to come by, he told himself, but I as soon they hadn't. Too much like paying a last visit to a friend that's going to join the silent majority pretty soon.

The glare was fading from the rocks around him, and the bite of the sun was less sharp. I guess this is it, he thought. My eyes is starting to give out, and I can't feel much no more. Little while, and everything'll just stop, I guess. Don't appear that it's going to be specially painful, anyhow. Had I of gone to church some, I'd have some words to go with this, but I don't expect it matters much, now, does it? Appears I'll have to be my own undertaker; shall I find a nice spot and lie down, get my arms crossed all proper? Shit to that, I'll keep on whiles I can.

He was snapped out of his reverie by what sounded like a cannon shot, and looked up to see that the reason for the dimming light was a bank of clouds that now covered most of the sky, roiling and undulating in a slow swirl of pearl-gray and near-black. Another thunderclap and a glare of lightning followed, then something white hit the ground ahead of him and shattered. In a moment he was being pelted with hailstones, but an overhanging rock nearby offered some protection.

Sheltered under it, he watched the hailstones, some of them the size of plovers' eggs, land and pile up. He reached out and snatched up a handful and sucked them greedily, savoring first their chill in his mouth, and then the trickle of water down his throat that their melting released.

After a few minutes, the hail gave way to a steady downpour of rain, which quickly filled a basinlike depression just outside his shelter. He cupped his hands, scooped up the water and drank, feeling life and strength return to his parched tissues.

By sunset the storm drifted off to the north, and night fell with the chill suddenness of the desert. His near-mortal thirst slaked, Faro was now at liberty to be aware of a consuming hunger and the throbbing pains in his feet. He eased his boots off and massaged his feet as best he could, then limped to another rain-filled depression in the rock and bathed them.

Under the shelter of the overhang, he curled himself up as tightly as he could manage to conserve his body's warmth. He prepared himself for sleep by trying to work out the meaning of what had happened to bring him to this place and this condition.

Somebody wanted him dead, was the main thing. Him and Mehitabel, in fact.

He was trying to worry out the who and the why of it when sleep caught up with him.

By midmorning, most of the puddles of rainwater had dried up, but there were still a few mouthfuls to be found here and there, and Faro moved along briskly and with renewed optimism. The character of the country was changing now, with some sparse vegetation to be found instead of bare rock. In the distance he could see patches of dusty green that might be grass. Somewhere along here, if anywhere in this godforsaken country, was where he might find people.

Shortly before noon, he did. He was working his way along the rim of a canyon when he spotted a group of a half-dozen figures ahead, some mounted, some afoot. He was about to break into a run and hail them when he paused and looked more closely at the gathering. One man appeared to have a noose around his neck and to be standing with arms bound behind him.

Faro decided that these men had best be approached cautiously. People who are about to perform a hanging are usually convinced of the justice of the act, but are often sensitive about uninvited witnesses. Under other circumstances, he would as soon have gone in another direction; but this crowd, lynchers or not, were his only hope for finding a way out of this deathtrap.

There was a stand of brush along the canyon rim, and he eased his way through it until he was within twenty yards of the group, well within earshot.

"Suggs," one man was saying to the bound man, "you have been caught, clear and undeniable, in horse stealin', and we have tracked you and caught you with the goods. You got anything to say for yourself?"

"I borrered it," the man said sullenly. "I would of put it back, and all fed and curried, too, Colonel."

The colonel shook his head. "Maybe, just maybe, Suggs. But that's only my horse. What about Myers's and Gotch's that we found at your hideout, that's been missing a couple weeks?"

"They must of run off on their own, an' come to where I was on account of the waterhole," Suggs said.

"See, they was both lamed up some, and I wanted to get 'em back in shape before as I took 'em back."

The colonel shook his head once more. "Suggs, you haven't got the brains for honest work, and it don't appear that you've got the talent to make a go of horse stealin', so I will have to say that we're doin' you a favor today. There's nothin' you're good for in this world, so you're better out of it. You're goin' to hang."

"From what?" Suggs said peevishly. "There ain't no trees around here, which without a tree nor a gallows you can't have no hangin'. If you're so set on this, whyn't you all ride on to where there's some trees and do it proper?"

"Don't worry about that," the colonel said. "Gotch!" A man in the group turned and unslung a bundle from a standing horse, then upwrapped it, revealing a large grindstone. He rolled this across the ground to where the trailing end of the rope around Suggs's neck lay, passed the end through the grindstone's center hole and lashed the rope firmly to the stone.

"Amos Suggs," the colonel said sternly, "may God have mercy on your soul, 'cause *we* are damned well fed up with you."

He nodded, and Gotch picked up the grindstone and pitched it over the rim of the canyon. The rope snapped taut, and Suggs was jerked into the air, somersaulting over the rock edge and out of sight. He had gone silently, and Faro hoped that the first jerk of the rope had broken his neck.

There came the sound of a distant impact of rock on rock, and the hanging party drifted to the edge of the canyon and looked down. "Stone's all broke, too," Gotch observed. "All right, though. It was pretty well wore out."

Faro decided that he would as soon not introduce himself to this crowd. They might take him for an accomplice of the late Suggs; and, even though they had used up their rope and grindstone, doubtless they could think of something equally final if they decided he was guilty of that or some other offense. He would, he concluded, wait until they left, then follow their trail to whatever passed for civilization hereabouts. With all those horses, there would be enough droppings to track them by, even if their hoofs left no trace on the rocky soil.

He turned to move a little further off, but, weaker than he had realized, stumbled against a rock and sent it clattering.

"Somebody in the brush," one of the men called, and in a moment they were standing around him.

"What we got here?" the colonel asked. "Another horse thief?"

"Wouldn't seem so," another man put in, "as he ain't got no horse."

"Maybe it's tethered somewheres a little away from here," the colonel said. "You got a horse, fellow? If you do, you'd best have a bill of sale for it."

Faro gestured at his battered, scarred boots. "If I had a horse, I'd of been riding it, not using up shoe leather on these damn rocks. I been afoot above a day out in the Badlands, and near as anything got fried to a crisp by the sun and dried out like a prune. A mercy I found you, gents."

"How come you didn't make yourself known?" the colonel asked suspiciously.

"Ah . . . you seemed busy, and I didn't want to interrupt," Faro said.

"How'd you come to be a-wanderin'?" Gotch asked.

"Was out with some . . . friends, some ways north of here," Faro said, "and we was jumped by Indians. My horse run off, then dumped me out in the middle of nowhere, and I been walking ever since to get back to somewhere." He stopped, feeling suddenly light-headed, and slumped to the ground.

He was vaguely aware of his boots being drawn from his swollen feet, and of a low whistle as the onlookers inspected them.

"This fellow ain't fit to travel back to wherever he's from," the colonel pronounced. "He'll need some rest and tendin'. Who'll stand ready to that?"

Faro heard a stir of muttering, which seemed to amount to the fact that none of those present had the the time or facilities to offer such care. "The Widder McCann's the nearest spread to here," one man said. "She c'd tend him proper, I expect."

"A good soul, Miz McCann," the colonel said approvingly. "That's the ticket—we'll drop him off with her."

Faro, still in a daze, was led to one of the horses— probably, he supposed, part of Suggs's unlawful estate —and helped onto it.

As it moved off, with him clutching desperately at the saddle horn, he heard Gotch say, "I b'lieve Miz McCann's got a spare grindstone; I'll see can I trade her something for it."

CHAPTER 9

"When they said the Widow McCann, I'll allow that I got a picture in my mind that was some different from what you are, ma'am," Faro said. "Lady on the shady side of fifty, constructed along the lines of a bolster and addicted to making calf's-foot jelly."

Mrs. McCann smiled at him briefly as she refilled his mug with steaming tea. "Any woman can be a widow, Mr. Blake. All you need to do is get married and have your husband die. It's very simple."

She was a tall, stately woman, perhaps five years Faro's junior, with dark-blonde hair coiled at the top of her head, and clad in a light woollen dress that draped her body clingingly enough to reveal its generous but not obtrusive contours. Her hair seemed to Faro almost like a crown; there was something queenly about her and the graceful calm of her movements.

"I'm sorry not to offer you anything stronger than tea, Mr. Blake," she said, "but I don't keep spirits in the house, not since my husband died. He wasn't a drinker to start with, but, out here where it's so desolate and lonely, he turned to it; and, in the end, it killed him. I know I could go that road myself if I had it on hand

—something to get through the nights and the days without a soul to talk to—so I don't have it."

"I wonder you stay on," Faro said. "You got some nice land down by the creek here, and stuff seems to be growing on it, but I don't see there's a living in it, especially if you got to handle it all on your own."

Mrs. McCann shrugged. "Jim put every cent we had into fitting out this place, the house, the tools, the animals. If I stay on another three months, and work at farming it, even if it doesn't bring in enough to make any money, the homestead grant will be confirmed, free and clear, and I'll be able to sell it to someone who can work it at a profit. It's hard, but I can stick it out."

"Would think it was some dangerous," Faro said. "There's Indians roving about all the time, and I'd think a lone woman would have something to worry about."

"They've never given me any trouble," she said, biting into a sweet biscuit with strong white teeth. "The colonel and those others that brought you in, they're all the time in a fever about the menace of the murdering heathen and all that trash, but that's mostly because they'd like the free use of all the land around here without worrying who it's supposed to belong to. The Indians come by now and then, and I give them a little tobacco or a cup of tea and a cake, and they go off peaceable as you please."

Faro took another sip of his tea, regretting Mrs. McCann's teetotal principles, and winced as his battered body reacted with another twinge, this time in his back. The sturdy wooden kitchen chair on which he was sitting was designed for people in reasonable health, not someone who'd been worn out, dried out and pretty nearly killed. He wasn't sure whether his head—where there were still a couple of lumps, either from his kidnapers' attentions or from the fall from the bolting horse—or his feet hurt the worst. The rest of the body wasn't in such good shape, either, but the feet and the head were the main sources of trouble.

Mrs. McCann noted his reaction and said, "Good heavens, I'm supposed to be tending you, so I'd best get to it. Let's have a look at your feet."

Faro gritted his teeth as she peeled his socks away; they had fused with his flesh, what with sweat, sores and burst blisters, enough so that the operation wasn't far off being skinned.

"They are a mess," Mrs. McCann said. "I don't know how you walked as far as you did on them."

"Was out of my head part of the time," Faro said. "If I'd of been in my right mind, somewheres along in that walk, I'd of lay down and died."

"Best thing is to soak them," Mrs. McCann said. "Do you think you're up to a short ride?"

"More than what I am to a short walk," Faro said cautiously. "You got to ride to your bathtub hereabouts?"

"In a way," she said, smiling. "Here, you slip on a pair of Jim's wool socks; that'll be enough, since you won't need your boots for riding. I'll go get the horses and bring them around to the front porch, so you won't have to walk far."

"Got a spare horse, do you?" Faro asked.

She turned to him with a look, not quite of sadness but of acceptance of what had happened and what her life had become. "Mr. Blake, I have a spare *everything* around here. Dishes for two, clothes for two, room for two. When someone dies, they don't take their gear along with them. What's left is there to be used."

"Now, that is something in the tub line," Faro said admiringly. After a steep but short ride up the rock slope above the McCann farm, he and Mrs. McCann surveyed a landscape that looked as though it belonged to another planet rather than the carefully tended creek-bed land below. The rock formations here had not been sculpted by wind and water, but by the deposit of rock that seemed to have bubbled out of the earth, creating fantastic forms streaked with vivid colors. At some distance, steam broke from the earth every few moments, accompanied by a heavy plopping sound. There was a pungent scent in the air, a slight taint of rotten eggs, but not strong enough to be actively unpleasant.

In front of where they stood, having just dismounted, was a basin perhaps eight feet by ten and, as far as Faro could judge, about four feet deep, filled with slightly murky water from which a thin mist of steam rose.

"Sit on the edge and roll your trouser legs up," Mrs. McCann said. "That's mineral water, naturally hot, and it'll soak the aches out of your feet in no time."

Faro followed her directions and was astonished at how quickly the cramping pains in his feet were soothed away.

"Hey, Ma'am," he said, "if you was to turn your back or move off some ways away, I could give myself a all-over soak in this, which I expect would do me a world of good."

"There's something better than that," she said. "If your feet are feeling all right, pull on the socks and come over here with me."

She led him to an area which he surveyed with disfavor. It was where he had observed the puffs of steam and heard the plopping sound, and, on close inspection, turned out to be a bed of mud about the size of a pool table, smelling strongly and emitting bubbles of gas.

"That looks like something a horse or cow wanders into and ain't never heard of again," he said.

"It looks bad and smells bad," Mrs. McCann said,

"but it's wonderful for making you feel good. It's warm, wet and thick, and clings around you 'til you feel . . . well, fine. Don't be afraid of it."

"I guess it is good that I am feeling so bad," Faro said, "else I wouldn't hanker for it on no account. But if you say she'll do me good, why, I'm for that."

Mrs. McCann moved away and out of sight behind an outcropping. Faro stripped and eased himself into the steaming mud, testing gingerly until he found a firm place to light on. It lapped up to his chin and stank fiercely; but after a moment he found he did not mind the smell. Maybe, he thought, something that awful had to be good for you.

The warm mud engulfed him, and he was conscious of a feeling of physical pleasure for the first time in days. Moved by the sluggish currents that kept it heated, it surged gently against his body, and the sense of pleasure became quite specific. As his erection grew, he had the sensation of penetrating warm moistness. . . .

"Enjoying it?" Mrs. McCann said from just above him. He gave a startled thrash in the mud, then realized that nothing of him from the neck down was visible, though his face was probably betraying something of what he was feeling.

"It is something different, I will tell you," he said. "I feel like a new man already."

"I know," she said. "I come up here a couple of times a week, and it always does me good."

I bet it does, Faro thought, looking at her with interest. Men's and women's bodies had their differences, but what that mud was doing to him couldn't help but be pretty close to what it did to or for her.

"I haven't been here for some days now," she said.

"It's a shame you had the trouble of the trip, and only me to have the benefit of it," Faro said carefully.

She looked at him as if she could see through the mud to where his erection twitched and throbbed as the warm, oozing mud caressed it. "If you were to close your eyes a moment, I could undress and get in at the other side," she said. "Then I'd be covered up just as much as you are, so it'd be all right."

"They are closed tight," Faro said. To his disappointment, she moved around behind him—after all, a man in a weakened condition can't be expected to force his eyelids shut so firmly that a little light or hint of motion can't seep through.

There was a sound of rustling cloth, then a squinting glimpse of a white form moving to the other side of the mudbed and disappearing slowly into it. "You can open your eyes now, Mr. Blake," Mrs. McCann said, with a touch of amusement in her voice.

The queenly blonde head was protruding from the surface of the mud, perhaps six feet away. It struck Faro as weird that there were two seemingly disembodied heads facing each other, with the rest of them out of sight—but sharing the same delicious warmth and moisture. He imagined the enfolding touch of the mud on Mrs. McCann's robust breasts and thighs, and between them. . . .

And she would damn well know what he was feeling, too.

He felt a touch against his shin. "Sorry," Mrs. McCann said. "I was trying to find an easier place to sit, and I must have slipped."

"Thass all right," Faro said thickly. "I'll scrooch over and make some room."

He moved, skidded and almost sank under the mud. He flailed wildly, then felt a firm hand grip his arm, and sat up.

"You want to be careful," Mrs. McCann said. Her effort to rescue him had brought her to an upright sitting position, exposing her mud-coated upper body. Her hand was still clutching his arm, apparently careless of the fact that the gesture brought it into contact with the side of one breast; it was gritty to the touch, but springily yielding.

"I don't know as careful is just what I want right now," Faro said, and brought his other hand up to cup her breast. It was fascinating, like touching a statue made of living earth

"Ah." Mrs. McCann leaned to him, open-mouthed. They kissed, and the warmth and moisture of her mouth was both similar to and different from the warmth and moisture of the mud. He moved his body against hers and felt her hand on his erection.

He was wondering how the business was to be managed—wonderful though the mud felt, he could see it had drawbacks when it came to fucking—when she stood up and stepped out of the mudbed.

"Not here," she said. "Come on." She walked lightly, almost running back to the pool where he had bathed his feet, looking from behind as if she were clad in a skin-tight brown suit. Faro followed more slowly on still-sore feet, feeling both excited and foolish, with the mud drying—a prickly, drawing sensation—on his body and his wagging erection.

When he got to the pool she was already in it, the mud dissolving in a cloud from her body, revealing its warm-white tint, the rosy nipples and the dark triangle between her thighs; she lay on her back, legs apart, arms spread.

Faro lowered himself into the pool and let the mud wash away from him; he gasped at the heat of the water, which seemed to him as hot as he could stand. It was fine on the feet, but all over was a different matter. He wondered if his erection could maintain itself under the extreme change in temperature.

He need not have worried. Mrs. McCann's touch brought it to throbbing life as she drew it into her. Buoyed by the density of the mineral water, she floated briefly on its surface, then sank under his weight until they reached an equilibrium somewhere between the surface and the bottom, with their heads above water.

As he thrust into her, the force of the action moved her away, so that they bobbed in the water; then, as he pulled back, her body followed his.

"Not like in a bed," she murmured, and caught his buttocks firmly in her hands, pressing herself against him. He reached behind her and did the same.

He scrabbled for a foothold on the bottom of the pool, found it, and pushed himself and her against its rim, thrusting hard now with something to push against. Mrs. McCann moved her pelvis against his, and hooked a leg around the small of his back, drawing him more firmly to her and changing the angle of his penetration with such an effect that he came at once. As his spasms subsided, he felt the fluttering clenching of her own response.

He eased his chest away from hers, careful to keep the contact at the loins; his penis was dwindling now, but still pleasantly sheathed. Mrs. McCann's head rested on the rim of the pool. Her breasts broke the surface of the water, and he bent to kiss the now-softened nipples that he remembered poking at his chest during their passion. They stiffened again under his tongue, and their taste was strange in his mouth—the bite of the mineral-laden water, not the ripeness of a woman with her own natural scents. He wondered what Mrs. McCann would be like out of the water . . . and was pretty sure he would be finding out.

"Hey, don't wriggle. You're distracting me; I almost ran the needle into my thumb."

"I ain't wriggling, *it* is," Faro said. "I am stone-still and comfortable, and admiring your skills at making and mending, along with the rest of you. And that is enough admiring to make any man's cock give a twitch now and again."

They were seated in a plush chair in the front room of the McCann farmhouse—more accurately, Faro was seated in the chair, and Mrs. McCann was seated on Faro, facing him and straddling his lap, securely, if quietly, joined to him. Faro was naked—out of necessity, as Mrs. McCann was mending the worst of the rents in his clothing caused by his desert wanderings. Mrs. McCann was also naked, without any compelling reason, but Faro did not feel inclined to complain. Watching a woman sewing had never struck him as an absorbing activity, but, this way, he saw that it had aspects he had not been aware of. If all housework could be done like this, he thought dreamily, lots of ladies would be a lot more interested in it. He speculated on how that would work out with dishwashing. Woman at the dishpan, wearing only an apron; man behind her— woman might have to be on a stool if she was short— man reaching around to dry a dish now and then, or run his hand under the apron front, give a slow squeeze or a stroke. . . .

"Hey! You're twitching so, I can't keep my fingers steady, and your mending'll never get done."

"It could wait for a bit," Faro said hoarsely. "Way I'm feeling, I don't believe this'll take long." He slid his hands under her buttocks and lifted her gently, then let her weight descend on him again. She dropped the clothing, the spool of thread and the needle to the floor and began moving against him, her head thrown back and her lower lip caught in her teeth. The scent of their coupling was warm and familiar, unlike the mineral smell of the pool. But that hadn't been bad at all, at all. In fact, nothing about Mrs. McCann was bad—looking at it fairly, she was about the best he had ever had, and seemed to have lots of ideas yet to try out.

He found himself wondering what it would be like to spend some time here—maybe even a lot of time. He was no farmer, but it couldn't be too hard to learn how to do it; and there wasn't much a man could buy with however much money he earned any other way that was a hell of a lot better than what he was getting right now.

The morning of the day after next, he was thanking his stars that he hadn't broached any such notions to Mrs. McCann. As he mended, the restlessness that was bone-deep in him returned, and he knew he would never be content with one place, or one woman, for long. Drifting around the lousier part of the frontier, pitting his skill and luck against the kind of man you found there might not be much of a life, but it was the one he knew, and the one that seemed to fit him.

Also, he saw now that Mrs. McCann would likely only have been embarrassed if he had suggested anything permanent to her. She had enjoyed him mightily, that was clear—there was a session, the day before, that had begun in her bed and finished on the front porch, leaving a trail of disarranged furniture and a torn curtain, that would stick in his memory as long as he lived—but she was showing signs that she considered these days an interlude in the main course of her life.

One such sign was what she was now saying over breakfast: "You're about well now, so I expect you'll be on your way soon." This was said in a matter-of-fact tone that seemed to leave no room for regret.

"I don't have to just yet," Faro said.

"You'll have things of your own to see to." Mrs.

McCann did not ask what they might be; in fact, Faro thought, she knew damned little about him, aside from how he was in bed—or in the pool, the mud bath, the chair, the porch and on the hearthrug. She was endlessly inventive and accomplished at lovemaking, but not much at loving, Faro suspected. Fine; that about summed him up in that line, too.

She looked up from her plateful of bacon and out the kitchen window. "Indians," she said. "Four of 'em, heading for the house."

"You got a gun some place?" Faro said.

"I do, but no need. I've seen a couple of 'em before, and they're friendly."

Faro was dubious, and peered past her at the approaching men. They weren't, so far as he could tell, painted for war, which was a good sign; but who said that an Indian had to be painted up before he took a notion to kill someone?

Mrs. McCann went to the kitchen door to greet them, then stepped hastily back into the room as the leader of the party elbowed his way in, staring at her intently.

Two of his followers stepped between Mrs. McCann and Faro, glaring at him. Both carried rifles which, possibly accidentally, had their barrels pointed in his direction.

"What on earth . . . ?" Mrs. McCann said faintly as the Indian leader reached for the top of her head, pulled out the restraining hairpins, and unwound the long coil of her hair to its full length. He turned and spoke in triumphant gutturals to his companions, slapping the long knife belted at his side for emphasis.

These is some friendly Indians, Faro thought. One day they'll settle for tea and little cakes, the next, they're fixing to scalp her alive. Well, I guess I got to put a stop to that shit. Let's see, I grab them two rifle barrels, one in each hand, and turn 'em aside, kick the chief in the balls with my right foot, and the fourth one with my left—no, then I got no feet to stand on and I'm dumped on my ass—the fourth one I lunge at and bite the nose off of or something . . . that is *some* plan, Blake.

Doomed as he knew it was, he tensed to make his move.

CHAPTER 10

With his fists clenched and his knees flexed, prepared to do the most damage he could before being shot dead, as he certainly would be, Faro paused. The two Indians with the rifles pointed at him were guffawing, and the third was looking sheepish, or possibly mulish. At the leader's barked command, he ventured over to Mrs. McCann and placed the edge of his left palm atop her scalp, and the edge of the right one on top of its fellow, then moved the left hand up to rest on the right. He repeated this climbing process until he had reached the end of Mrs. McCann's tresses, still held outstretched by the leader.

"White woman's hair twelve hands long, like I say," the leader said. "You say ten only, Dog Walks Sideways, so I win. T'ank you, Mo-kan," he added, turning to Mrs. McCann. "This fellow bet with me how long your hair. I say twelve hands, he say ten. So we measure, yes?, and I win many ponies, me, Eagle Claw. And two buffalo robes, fur side outside."

"Well, I guess you have a better eye for hair than your friend, then," Mrs. McCann said, moving away from Eagle Claw as he let her hair drop. "But I will say, you have a kind of sudden way of seeing who wins a bet."

"Haw," Eagle Claw said. "Dog Walks Sideways never have chance, dumb like an Assiniboin." From the glower with which the losing bettor greeted this comment, and the snickers it elicited from the other two Indians, Faro assumed that the quartet were Tetons, mortal enemies of the Assiniboin and therefore prone to make them the butt of any derogatory comment. "Me, Eagle Claw, I see Mo-kan up the hill once, wash self in hot water with hair down, and it cover half ass—so *have* to be twelve hands, maybe twelve and one."

"Lord almighty," Mrs. McCann said, "you mean you watched me while I was taking a bath up there? That's . . . that's . . . well, you shouldn't have done it, Eagle Claw—that's a bad thing."

"Heeee," Eagle Claw said dispiritedly. "White people want to pretend don't wash? Always something whites say do, say don't, and nothing make sense. When we get back to village, Eagle Claw be rich, Dog Walks Sideways piss-poor, though; that main thing."

Faro recalled the Indian propensity to bet hugely on just about anything, from games of chance to which of three flies would first leave a fresh buffalo chip. He had never cared to practice his trade among them, though; they tended to be short on cash, which on prinicple he preferred to play for. Winning a stake such as Dog Walks Sideways had just lost might elate Eagle Claw, but realizing its value would be more trouble than it was worth to a professional gambler. Also, their favored games were often complex, involving mathematical calculations that were beyond him.

Mrs. McCann said, "Your village is up near the Missouri, isn't it, Eagle Claw?" At the Indian's agreement, she turned to Faro and said, "You told me that professor's camp was about a day's wagon trip north and west of Deadwood, didn't you?"

Faro nodded, reflecting that it was surprising that in the preceding frenzied nights and days he had had time to chat with his hostess, but in the quieter moments he had, in fact, been able to tell something of where he had been and what had happened.

"Well, then," she said, "that's a way for you to get back there. There's no stages or such running hereabouts, and you surely wouldn't want to try to make your own way back; but you could travel with Eagle Claw and his friends, and be near enough there in a couple of days so's you could make it easily."

She was very matter-of-fact about it, and the assumption that it was time for Faro to be on his way was too clear to be missed. Eagle Claw, expansive in his victory, agreed to the proposition; and, after a breakfast of Mrs. McCann's tea and cakes, the Indians rode off with Faro.

He was mounted on Mrs. McCann's spare horse, purchased with two of the three ten-dollar gold pieces he had found in an inside pocket, overlooked by his recent captors. He made sure to insist on a bill of sale, carefully written out and describing the horse in detail. He did not expect to run across the colonel, Gotch and the rest again, but there was no use not being prepared.

"This man you with, he dig up stone bones?" Eagle Claw asked. Faro found the conversation tedious, especially after continuing for some hours of riding across the broken country, but Eagle Claw seemed determined to extract the maximum entertainment value from his guest, and persisted in questioning him.

"Yeah," Faro said.

"Why? Stone bones been there many men's lives, old

animals that ain't no more. No good for making medicine for hunting; none of them left to hunt."

"He teaches about them in a school back east," Faro said.

"I went to school once, Fathers ran it," Eagle Claw said. "Learned to speak English good, count, where Austria-Hungary is, things like that. What good to learn about old bones?"

"It's a thing white men like to do," Faro said.

"I think in white men's schools, they got special teaching how to cheat Indians."

"I wouldn't say that," Faro protested. "But, of course," he went on, doubtful of his ability to change Eagle Claw's views, "I wouldn't know, never having been to school myself."

"They got to learn it some place, why not school?" Eagle Claw said. "Maybe you speak straight, but I think that teacher man you with, he after yellow lead. When whites dig, it yellow lead they looking for, you bet."

"Not the kind of country for it, way I understand it," Faro replied. "Gold in the Black Hills, sure, but not out in the Badlands. No, the Professor's set on his bones and nothing else. He's got stories about them creatures that'd amaze you, like the one that had two brains, one for the front end and one for the hind."

Eagle Claw relished, though clearly without crediting, what Faro could dredge up of Fenn's description of the nature and lives of the dinosaurs, evidently regarding him as a talented, if untrustworthy, story-teller.

When Faro finally touched on the rivalry with Professor Handel, Eagle Claw was able to accept something of the account. "Not the old bones that matter," he decided, "but the fight, now that make sense. Men

want to fight, they find something to fight about, so old
bones as good as anything else."

Camp for the night was near a rare Badlands creek,
where Eagle Claw and his party found another half-
dozen of their fellow-tribesmen, also homeward bound.
There were already two skin tents erected, and Eagle
Claw and his men put up another pair. Among the
tethered horses, Faro noticed a small spotted dog running loose, and barking cheerfully as it avoided the
occasional hoof-blow aimed at it.

After the evening meal, a kind of stew made mainly
of dried beef and herbs, Faro was invited by Eagle
Claw to tell his tales of Fenn's fabulous monsters,
which were received with appreciation, winning him
several puffs at the red-stone pipe which was passed
around with great ceremony. Whatever they were smoking was nothing like a good Pittsburgh stogie, but left
him a little light-headed, as if he had had a belt or so
of very smooth bourbon.

"Haw," one Indian said, after Faro had described
the fearsome allosaurus, "sound like Indian agent. Eat
everything that move, and too big to kill."

"I hear they are a sorry lot, mostly," Faro said.
"Not that I ever have any dealings with them, you
understand. But they tell me there is, maybe, some new
ones coming along that will be more on you people's
side, treat you fair and all that." He thought of Simon
Buckthorn and his ambitions to be the model of what
an Indian agent should be. It would be nice if some
official gave the Indians a better view of whites than
they had had. It was not very comfortable to travel
among people who seemed to have every right to dis-
like anyone who looked the way you did.

From Buckthorn his mind drifted to Melissa Chapman and her interest in championing Buckthorn's cause.

How she proposed to do that by reporting on Fenn's diggings he couldn't imagine. It would be interesting to see her again, anyhow, if she were still there.

"New ones, old ones, same," an old man said. "What Indians get from whites, one way, another, kills. Gunpowder, rifles, we hunt better, but kill each other better too. Whiskey, make you feel good but make you crazy, do things give whites right to hang you. Even blankets to keep warm. . . ." The old man looked into the fire. "Me, I Mandan," he said. "Once Mandan big tribe, strong, other Sioux respect us. We had fine towns, rich, time for dancing and games. Then, back when I little boy, white men come, trade us warm blankets, pretty colors. Everybody like, everybody have, everybody use. And most everybody die. Some of them traders, they had the smallpox, and blankets they trade us carry it. First some Mandan get it and die; then other Mandan get it from them and die; and soon almost all Mandan dead. Now I live with Tetons. They fine people," he said with a swift look around the circle, "but not Mandan. Hard to have wife die, harder to have son die. Most of my life I spend feeling how hard to have whole people die. So I think, what whites give, kills."

As Faro was composing himself for sleep in the crowded tent he shared with two of Eagle Claw's party, he heard an outraged yip, presumably from the puppy he had seen running among the horses. In the morning he became aware of the reason for this as, rising just at dawn, he wandered by the cook-fire and saw a man stirring the contents of a pot with a long stick.

"What's that?" Faro asked.

"Breakfast," the man said. "Boiled dog. Good eating, nice and fat."

"Sounds so," Faro said. "I believe I will take me a

walk so as to work up a appetite for it." He walked away from the camp into the morning mists. Behind him the only visible figure was the cook; the other Indians still slept in their tents after a long night of talking and smoking.

Faro had no intention of returning to camp until after the breakfast treat had been consumed. He was rarely a hearty eater in the morning, favoring an egg beaten up in brandy—and in a pinch doing without the egg. Boiled dog was a delicacy he could deny himself.

He climbed the rocky slope above the creekside camp, savoring the moist chill of the morning; soon enough, the rising sun would burn off the mists and signal the start of another glaring Badlands day, with any luck the last full one he would spend on his journey back to Fenn's camp.

The mist was so thick that he could see only a few feet in front of him; he seemed to be moving in a small room that presented new terrain to his feet as he walked, rocks and bushes emerging from the gray wall in front of him and vanishing behind.

He heard the twitter of an early bird-song—then another sound, a metallic jingling. Then there came the snort of a horse.

For an instant he wondered if he were approaching a party of hostile Indians—Assiniboin or Cree, or whoever else didn't care for Tetons—then realized that mounted Indian warriors didn't jingle.

He moved forward cautiously; then, suddenly, the mist thinned, and he was confronting a blue-clad figure on a black horse, who was eyeing him with considerable interest and holding a cavalry carbine pointed at his midsection.

Behind the trooper the thinning mist revealed about a dozen and a half others. Three of them were grouped around a stocky man on a bay horse who seemed to have trouble keeping his seat in the saddle.

It was a little too far to recognize the face, but the attitude made it, for Faro, a ten-to-one bet that he had once more encountered Captain Meyner.

CHAPTER 11

"Where'd you come from?" the trooper asked. "Down there, the Indian camp?"

"Uh, yes," Faro said, doubting he could make a convincing case for having been in the Badlands on his own. "They're guiding me up to some place west of Deadwood. Took a notion to have me a stroll before breakfast."

"You picked a damn good time for it," the trooper said, "but maybe not the best place to promenade to. Come on over this way, the captain'll want to see you. What he can make out of you, anyhow," he added sardonically. "Vision ain't so good just now."

"Boozed again, is he?" Faro asked, starting to move as the trooper had directed. The cavalryman moved his horse along slowly, pacing Faro.

"You know Captain Meyner?" the trooper asked.

"Of him. Plus which I traveled with him on the stage into Deadwood 'bout a week ago."

"He'll know you, then," the trooper said. "That's probably lucky, considering where you come from just now. He's of a mind to be sudden about folks that hang out with Indians."

"Shit," Faro said. "He was passed out the whole time, doubt he ever saw me. Slept through an Indian attack on the coach, in fact."

The trooper was amused. "Way he told it after he got back to the unit, he took personal charge after the driver and passengers panicked, and druv 'em off with heavy losses all by himself."

Meyner, when the trooper brought Faro up and stated where he had come from, peered blearily at him, swaying perilously in his saddle, and said, "You a captive that's escaped from the murdering heathen, or some damn renegade that ought to be hung because he's too low for shooting?"

It was clear that these were the only two categories in which the captain was capable of placing him, and Faro said firmly, "Captive, sir. They took me unawares some south of here and was meaning to sacrifice me for good luck next Thursday. I gnawed my way loose from the ropes they tied me with and run off whiles they was still asleep."

"Good, good," Meyner said vaguely. "You tell the sergeant here about their forces and such. Good source intelligence preparation attack."

"Sir," the sergeant, a tall, rawboned man with the look of someone who had seen combat for half his life, said, "this attack. . . . Sir, there's no sign from what we saw last night that that's anything but a peaceful camp, nothing hostile or anything—bar," he added with a curious look at Faro, "this business about captives and sacrifice, which I'll go into with this gentleman. But if we hit them like you say, it'll be Crow Creek all over again."

"Jusso," Meyner said. " 'Nother Crow Creek's what we need. Lots more good Indians." He chuckled.

"Begging the Captain's pardon, sir," the sergeant said, "and with respect, I got to say that Crow Creek got the Captain in a lot of hot water with the command and with the War Department. If the Captain will recollect, the Captain had to face an inquiry then, and it was a close business. If the Captain orders this attack, I can't see but what the Captain would get handled pretty rough."

"Different now, Sergeant," the captain said. "Friends in high places, see Meyner through, stand by him. Meyner's on the front lines, see, does what has to be done, and there's those that'll see him and his men don't suffer by it. Wipe out the red niggers, thass all we got to worry about, and here's a bunch for the wiping. You here," he added, looking again at Faro, "you wanna join in the attack, get revenge your wrongs? Shoot 'em, brain 'em, what you like, we'll give you horse, weapons."

"I as soon stay up here, sir," Faro said.

"Good idea," Meyner said, swaying once more, and suddenly eluding the grasp of the sergeant to topple to the ground from his mount. He tottered to his feet, pawing his horse's stirrups for support, and continued, "Stay up here as sniper, pick off any that run off when we hit 'em. Sergeant, go talk to this man, find out what he knows disposition enemy forces, report back me."

"Sir." The sergeant saluted, dismounted, and led Faro out of sight and earshot of the rest of the troop.

"Now, Mister, what's all this about captives and sacrifices? None of the Sioux've done that for years."

"Well, I lied," Faro said. "Seemed to me it was either that or extend a engraved invitation to my own hanging. Them Indians is guiding me to where I got to go, and, seems to me, that classes me as a renegade in Meyner's book. What is this shit about attacking them people? They're just drifting back to their village, meaning no harm to anyone."

"The captain's set on it," the sergeant said gloomily.

"I hate this kind of stuff. If you do it and it works, which usually means you got surprise and more men, then everybody yells massacre. And if it's a tougher fight than that, then you take casualties, and all for nothing. I don't mind going up against a war band, any size—I been fighting out here for years, and I know what to do and what to tell my men to do—but jumping camps and villages just to pile up dead that the captain can put in his reports, that ain't no job for a soldier. Lieutenant Mulhern could usually get him to think twice, but the captain put the lieutenant on report for hiding his whiskey, and so he's confined to quarters back at the base for this sweep. I'm second in command, but you see how much he listens to me."

"And he's got the bars on his shoulders, so you got to do what he says," Faro said.

"When he gives the order to attack in a couple minutes, we'll attack," the sergeant said sadly. "Even though there ain't a man among us that don't know it's plain murder. But if you don't obey an officer's order, why, then, you ain't got an army at all, do you?"

"Good point," Faro said. "You know," he went on after a moment of thought, "I ain't a army man myself."

"No, you ain't."

"So I don't have to pay that much attention to them bars. Could be I could have a talk with him, persuade him he's making a mistake."

"Could be," the sergeant said, clearly doubting it.

"Now, the captain said I was to be armed, didn't he?" Faro asked.

"So he did."

"So you'd be obeying his orders if you was to give me the lend of your revolver. A revolver," Faro said meaningfully, "has got a nice heavy butt onto it. It seems to me that if I was to go off somewhere private and talk with the captain, it might be that the drink would take him all over again, so's he wouldn't be able to give any orders and it'd be up to the man that's next in line to decide just what to do next."

The sergeant grinned and slipped his long-barreled revolver from its holster, then handed it to Faro. "It ain't loaded just now, but I don't expect that matters. It is wonderful how devious a civilian's thinking works. I would say you ain't got the military mind."

"I thank you most sincere for the compliment," Faro said.

"Now, you men," the sergeant said, "the captain has been took with one of his attacks, and is resting. Them Indians is going to move out before as he, uh, recovers, that's clear; and he wouldn't want us to go into the attack without his inspired leadership. So the job's off, and we'll move on the regular patrol route."

As the troopers dispersed to ready their mounts for departure, the sergeant turned to Faro. "You done that real neat," he said. "Couldn't even feel a bump on his head. Or maybe he really did pass out before you could . . . ?"

"You are free to think that," Faro said. "In any case, I doubt he'll wake up before an hour and a half." The heavy cavalry weapon had not had the easy heft in his hand of his familiar Reid's knuckleduster-pistol, but he thought he had gauged the force of the tap—it was all in the snap you gave the wrist at the last moment—and the spot, just aft of the right ear, pretty well. Captain Meyner, drunkenly anticipating some important piece of military intelligence that had to be discussed out of hearing of his subordinates, had folded quietly to the ground, and was now being arranged in a litter slung between two horses.

"You say you're going up to that professor man's camp west of Deadwood?" the sergeant said. "Our patrol route takes us about by there—whyn't you travel with us? We'd likely make better time than your Indians, and you'd be eating U.S. Army rations, which I expect beats the chow you'd get with them."

Faro, thinking of the boiled dog he had avoided at breakfast, had to agree. "But I'd think," he said, "that Meyner'd have a little something to say about that. I mean, it ain't every day that he gets took severely drunk whiles in the company of a civilian, and he could entertain low suspicions about that."

The sergeant looked grim. "I misdoubt that sponge he uses for a brain is much good for remembering," he said. "In any case, I been studying out this whole business. I promised Lieutenant Mulhern I'd do what I could to keep the captain from doing something foolish, and from ruining the, uh . . . well, shit, I don't like to say it, but it's the only word . . . honor of the troop. You done something I wouldn't of, and it's made me think. So you can figure it's okay for you to ride with us. Go on down and get your horse."

At the Indian camp, Faro was greeted with sour looks and ostentatiously displayed rifles and war-axes. Eagle Claw hailed him as he approached. "We see horse soldiers at top of hill—you come from them. They send you to tell us to surrender?"

"Give them answer they can understand," the old Mandan shrilled. "Cut Ba-laik's head off, put on pole, that how we surrender! Let the horse soldiers come at us—we show them how Teton die, how Mandan die! Also how white man die, this one, Ba-laik, first."

To forestall what appeared to be a favorable consideration of the old man's suggestion, Faro said hastily, "That is a interesting program, but there ain't no need for it. I spotted them soldiers early on this morning, and went up to palaver with them. So they know you are the peaceable kind of Indian, that don't wish them any ill—" the old Mandan spat into the dust "—and nor they don't you. So, if it's all right with you, I will take my horse and join up with them. They are going just about where I am supposed to end up, so it'll work out better that way."

Eagle Claw looked at him gravely. "I think we got to thank you," he said. "Seem to me, if you not go up and talk, maybe horse soldiers attack, catch us sleeping. Lucky that Meyner, that murdered all them at Crow Creek, not leading horse soldiers. Not so easy to talk then, I think."

"Well, he ain't," Faro said shortly. He thought it best not to mention that Meyner was present on the scene physically, if not wakefully; the proximity of the Butcher of Crow Creek might inspire the Indians to a suicidal attack on the cavalry, which would almost certainly get Faro Blake killed by one side or the other.

"We have thanks gift," Eagle Claw said. "Not much, but Indian not have much now. But is good piece of boiled dog left from breakfast. You eat before you go."

There seemed to be no way out of it. Faro knew enough of Indian pride to know that refusal of the offer would be a serious insult. He suggested hopefully that the delicacy be wrapped for consumption on the journey, but he was assured that boiled dog eaten cold or reheated was nothing like boiled dog freshly cooked, and would really be too mean a gift to sort with Teton generosity. So eat it here and now he must.

Actually, he told himself a few minutes later, wiping greasy fingers onto his trousers, it wasn't all that bad.

As he was preparing to mount his horse and leave the Indian camp, the faint sound of a distant shot drifted down from the top of the slope where the cavalry troop was gathered.

"What that?" Eagle Claw asked him.

"Somebody cleaning his gun, went off by mistake," Faro said with an ease he did not feel. "Nothing to worry about."

"The captain woke up, decided he wanted to clean his gun, only it turned out the damn thing was loaded, and it took the top of his head right off," the sergeant told Faro. "We ain't got ice nor spirits to pack him in, so we'll have to bury him right here. Later on, they can send out a undertaker's wagon to fetch him if they want."

"Tragic accident," Faro said.

"Yeah," the sergeant said. "Luckily I was nearby when he done it, though not in time to stop him, so I can testify to what happened. Nobody else was around, see?" He looked at Faro intently.

Faro thought he understood all too well. "Wouldn't of done for there to be any mystery about it," he agreed.

After the hasty burial and the insertion of a wooden marker—prudently omitting Meyner's name, so as not to invite desecration by a passing Indian—into the grave, the sergeant took careful notes of landmarks so that any retrieval of the body the Army might undertake would be possible; then the troop, with Faro and the sergeant bringing up the rear, moved out to the north.

As he rode, Faro considered that the military mind, in spite of its reputation for rigidity, could usually find the way to the solution of a problem. Whatever the sergeant might have on his conscience, he could truthfully say that he had never disobeyed a direct order.

CHAPTER 12

Arriving two days later at Fenn's camp, Faro was greeted by the professor with open arms and by Melissa Chapman with a firm handshake. He wished it had been the other way around. Although anybody who had spent the time he had with Mrs. McCann ought by rights to have used up his interest in women for a while, he found that she was still undeniably stirring to him.

"Tell me how you eluded the scoundrels, Blake," Fenn said. "Did they mistreat you?"

"Didn't get the chance. They had notions that way, from what they said, but some Indians jumped 'em and I got away. I expect they all got killed, so I can't say's I hold any grudge against 'em still."

"So many the fewer to do the rascal's work for him," Fenn said.

"Rascal?"

"Handel, of course," Fenn said. "Who else would exert such malignity? Tell me, Blake, did the ruffians who took you question you about our progress? Did you tell them of the allosaurus skeleton? No matter, after all, as the wretches had no chance to transmit anything they might have learned."

"I can't say as the matter come up," Faro said. "Listen, Professor, it truly don't seem to me that that Professor Handel was into that. Them fellows didn't seem as if they cared spit about dinosaur bones. They seemed some concerned about turning me into a fossil, maybe, but that's about as far as their interest in the topic went."

"He is slyer than you think, Blake," Fenn said. "Handel plays a deep game."

"I would say," Faro persisted equably, "that if Handel was out to do you harm, he'd have a try at you, or maybe some of the fellows that is best at digging for you, not me. I don't expect the work suffered from me being gone. So I'd be about the last person here he'd want to have taken out into the Badlands and corpsed."

"Ah, that's just what he'd *want* you to think," Fenn said.

Assured of Faro's well-being, the professor went off to supervise the day's digging—in Faro's absence, some prized minor bones of allosaurus had come to light, and the skeleton, save for the skull, was almost complete. Faro turned to Melissa Chapman. "You put any stock in that notion about Professor Handel being behind what was done to me?"

"Of course not," she said. "Professor Handel is a well-known scholar with an international reputation. Just like Professor Fenn, he's wholly absorbed in his specialty."

"He's some absorbed in Fenn, too, just like Fenn is in him," Faro said, and told her of his encounter with the German at the trading post. "With both of 'em so down on each other, you got to wonder if maybe one of 'em ain't right."

"I take it you haven't been to a university, Mr. Blake," Melissa Chapman said.

"A couple months, just before the War," Faro said. He did not enlarge on his college career. If Melissa Chapman wanted to think that he had dropped his education to serve one side or the other—rather than, as was the case, being kicked out for running a card game in his rooms—well, let her.

"Not long enough for you to take in what academic rivalry can do. When scholars disagree—or, worse, when they agree and are trying to get credit for having come up with whatever it is they agree on first—they can be as savage and merciless as an allosaurus. They use words rather than claws and fangs, but they're out to kill, all the same."

"Well, it wasn't words that was being used on me," Faro said. "Them fellows was out for the real thing, not talk. And they got some connection with Deadwood, from what they said. That Fowler, that took shots at me and Mehitabel—" he had mentioned the sniping incident, with some judicious editing of the actual circumstances, to her shortly after her arrival at Fenn's camp "—was in charge of 'em until he lucked out, and I got the idea that they was working for someone that wanted her and me dead. Though what for, I still can't puzzle out."

"There could be a number of reasons," Melissa Chapman said, in an offhand way. Something in her manner, though, gave Faro the distinct impression that she had a definite opinion on what those reasons might be—and that she had no intention of sharing it with him.

After dinner that night, Fenn insisted that Faro and Melissa Chapman join him in his tent for an urgent discussion.

"Direct assault is the only thing," he began.

Faro, who had been brooding through the evening meal over Melissa Chapman's lack of response to his overtures and had begun to feel that overt action rather than courtship might be more effective, started a little at what seemed to be a reading of his thoughts.

"Burn the villain out," Fenn went on. "Trounce him and his knavish crew so that they depart and trouble us no more—that's the course to follow. We have suffered enough of his outrages."

"You're proposing to raid Professor Handel's camp, Professor Fenn?" Melissa Chapman asked, with just enough stress on the academic titles to indicate how preposterous she considered the suggestion to be.

"To use the man's own barbarous tongue, *Ich kann nicht anders*—I can do no other."

"And if it worked," Melissa Chapman said, "you'd be left in charge of an allosaurus skull as well as an allosaurus skeleton. Very convenient."

"That has nothing to do with it," Fenn said hotly, "and I resent the imputation. The man's offenses reek to the heavens—the assaults on Blake here, and—"

"Professor," Faro cut in wearily, "I been trying to make you understand that the odds is just too long against Handel having anything to do with that. Now, you and this Handel man have got your arguments, and I guess there ain't no reason not to argue, if arguing's what you relish. But when you get to talking of setting up raids and such, I would say you are starting to slip your moorings. No, hear me," he went on as Fenn spluttered a protest, "I know you got some of this wrong about Handel already, and as a man that's trained in logic and grammar and all, you're long-headed enough to know there's some kind of chance you're wrong about the rest. I never care much to find some other gambler working a place I'd figured I had

a claim on, and if I could, I'd find a way to suggest
he move on. But I never made the mistake of telling
myself he was outfitted with horns and a tail and a
pitchfork—and if I had of, I wouldn't of rightly knowed
what I was up against. Out there in the Badlands, a
thing happened I didn't get a chance to tell you—was
some cavalry was set to jump some Indians, and them
same Indians ready to jump the cavalry, and it was
me that talked to both sides and made 'em see that they
didn't have nothing to fight about, or not just then."
Faro's vigorous revision of the event touched on reality
only lightly, but, coupled with some urging from
Melissa Chapman, seemed to have some softening effect
on the professor's attitude. The nice thing about a good
lie, Faro thought, is that you can shape it just right;
truth usually has a lot of rough edges that you can't
make fit in.

It was finally agreed that, if Faro could manage it,
the two professors would meet face to face and discuss
their differences and grievances as befitted rational men.

"But you will have to allow me the right to take action if it comes to nothing, as I confidently expect,"
Fenn said. "Almost every war is preceded by a peace
conference designed to prevent it. And how do you
propose to get to Handel, in any case? If you approached his camp, he would probably have you shot
like a dog."

"Out here, they don't shoot dogs, they boil 'em,"
Faro said. "Anyways, if I take on a job, you can bet
I'll work out a way to do it."

It seemed a safe assumption, though he did not feel
obliged to tell Fenn so, that the heat of noon would
drive Handel to the refuge of the trading post and the
unsatisfactory beer it offered.

*　　*　　*

"Way they are yelling, was I on a flatboat, I'd expect to see knives out and thumbs getting at eyeballs by this time," Faro said.

He and Melissa Chapman were seated at one rough, splintery table at the trading post. The two professors, one with a tumbler of whiskey, the other with a mug of beer in front of him, faced each other across another. It had taken all Faro's guile to persuade Handel to accept the meeting this evening; and now he was not sure it had been worth it.

"I think it's going well," Melissa Chapman said. She, like Faro, had chosen to sample the post's whiskey, and he had been interested to note that she drank it without any ladylike coughing or insistence on water. Her hand around the tumbler was fine-boned but strong-looking, and he had a sudden, vivid picture of it stroking and exploring him.

"They're having at each other hammer and tongs," she went on, "but it's shifted from them complaining about each other to arguing about paleontology. And you may have missed it, but just now Fenn said that he might have been wrong about the dentition of the trachodonts from Kansas."

"I guess I must of been distracted," Faro said. "That is a wonder, for sure."

"The thing is," Melissa Chapman said, "the poor souls haven't had anybody they regard as fully human to talk to out here—the diggers, you, me, we don't count because we're not academics. They may be deadly rivals, but at least they speak the same language, and they're enjoying it. It was quite something for you to get them together, Mr. Blake. I can see that in many ways you're a remarkable man."

"Well, now," Faro said, "I take that as a pretty encouraging sign."

"Don't," Melissa Chapman said. But there was a trace of a smile on her lips as she said it.

"It is all very well for you, Handel, to prate of your discoveries," Fenn said heatedly. "I grant that you've found some good things—I hope I'm open-minded enough to admit that. But really, my good man, that isn't science—given unlimited funds and a crew of expert diggers, acquired by means we need not go into, such as hiring them away from a colleague, any peasant could make such *discoveries*."

"Of course I hire your diggers," Handel said. "The ones I hired had vanished, doubtless eaten by wolves. I pass over the fact that their twin brothers now, it appears, are working on your site. And what do you mean, unlimited funds? Do you think the *Königlich-und-Kaiserlich* Treasury pours forth vast sums for sciences that neither make money for German industry nor advance the arts of the military? Let a man make a garish color out of coal tar, or invent a way to blow up hundreds rather than tens of his fellow-beings at once, and the purse-strings are loosened. But for so-foolish Handel and his old lizards, what comes is uncertain, late and doled out pfennig by pfennig. It is you Americans who have the bottomless pockets, as is well-known."

"The knowledge has escaped the trustees of Harvard University," Fenn said dryly. "They've given me the chair of paleontology, but damned little padding to put on it, so to speak, and I am getting a sore bottom. You wouldn't believe the dribble of funds I've had to work with this summer. All the money goes to trash like literature, law, Greek and Latin, astronomy, religion, grammar, art, history and so on."

"You too?" Handel said. "I had not known it was so."

"I don't mind telling you—well, yes I do, but, damn

it, I *will* tell you," Fenn said, "that I am about out of cash to pay my crew. If Miss Chapman over there can get some interesting stuff about my work into her magazine, it might turn the trustees' heads so they'd put up some more money, but that won't do me any good for this summer. It looks like I'll have to pack up and move out in a week or so for the rest of the season, and leave Lord knows what behind for you to come around and dig up. I'd half a mind to dynamite the beds before I left to spoil it for you, but I couldn't do that."

"No, you could not," Handel said gravely. "I know that, because I had such an idea much on my mind, and knew that it was, finally, not-to-be-thought-of. I too, you see, must soon abandon my diggings, and for the same reason as you. It is bitter, my dear Fenn, but what can we do?"

"What we can do, Professor Handel," Fenn said firmly, "is order another couple of portions of this swill—or these swills, as yours profanes the name of beer and mine that of whiskey—and numb our brains for the nonce."

"Well, they are friends enough now," Faro muttered to Melissa Chapman, "but it don't seem that it solves their problems after all. I guess I done what I could, so I will be moving on."

"Where to?"

"I can strike up to the Missouri, take a boat down-river to Omaha and do a good bit of business at the state fair there," Faro said. "There is a lot of people with money to spend on just about anything, and it'd be hard not to find a way of separating the one from the other."

"Do you enjoy making your living by fleecing people?" Melissa Chapman asked.

Faro refused to be irritated; he had come to realize that if you wanted to talk with Melissa Chapman, you had to be prepared to take a good deal of tartness in the dose. "It ain't fleecing," he said. "I give 'em what I tell 'em I will, a fair game for their money. They know I know the odds and the rules better than they do, and that's my only edge; and if they want to put their money down, why, it's their money to do it with. Now, if it's fleecing you want, you look at some of them fair attractions, like the mermaid that's a old dogfish and a stuffed monkey sewed together and showed as the real thing, and drawing in more money than a respectable gambler can clear any day."

"You may be right," Melissa Chapman said. She glanced at the next table, where the two professors were condoling with each other. "It's a shame, you know. I don't know or care anything, really, about dinosaurs, but those men are really dedicated, and there ought to be a way for them to do their work. It's harmless, at least, and there are mighty few jobs you can say that about—certainly not yours or mine."

"Onliest way for them to do what they want is to get their hands on a lump of cash in the next couple weeks," Faro said, "and that ain't . . . well, damn . . . if maybe . . . hell*fire*. Be something," he told Melissa Chapman, "if a man could help them two out of the spot they see themselves in, wouldn't it?"

"Something indeed," Melissa Chapman said, looking at Faro with what seemed to him the closest to an expression of female interest that he had yet encountered from her. "It would take an extraordinary man to do it, I'd think."

"Then watch one in action, ma'am," he said, and rose and walked to the professors' table.

"Gents," he said, "appreciate you setting me straight on what it is you been digging up this summer. My impression," he said to Professor Fenn, "is, you got about a whole skeleton of that allosaurus lizard, am I right?"

"None of the significant osseous structures are absent, yes," Fenn said.

"And you," Faro said to Handel, "got a whole skull and some?"

"I do," Handel said, obviously puzzled.

"And one of 'em isn't a baby or a dwarf or anything along them lines?"

The professors agreed that their specimens seemed to have come from mature individuals of approximately the same size.

"Then, gents and professors," Faro said, "I got a suggestion to make."

CHAPTER 13

"Are you sure that vertebra goes *just* there, my dear Fenn?"

"If not there, then quite near by, Handel. Do let me point out that I have had the advantage of observing the components of this skeleton *in situ,* so must claim a certain credence for my intuitions in these matters."

"To be sure, to be sure, my good Fenn. And in any case, this is but a temporary arrangement, eh?—fortunately, not one likely to be observed by any with more expertness than ourselves. If we are in error on some details, it will not be noticed by those who pay to see our allosaurus."

"No more it won't," Fenn said cheerfully. "And, by George, won't they just pay!"

Faro, standing with Melissa Chapman near the wall of the big tent erected on the Nebraska State Fair grounds on the outskirts of Omaha, grinned. They were watching the two professors busily wiring fragments of allosaurus to a massive form constructed of burlap draped over planking and barrel staves and supported on stout timbers driven into the hard-packed earth that floored the tent. "Seems like they have took to show business pretty quick," he said. "All that about science gets forgot when the cash comes into it."

"They'll justify it by saying they need the money to carry on their scientific work," Melissa Chapman said, "and that any little sloppiness doesn't matter alongside that."

"Well, that was the main idea," Faro said.

"And, I have to say, a good one—really brilliant," Melissa Chapman observed.

Faro's suggestion, at the trading post peace conference, that Fenn and Handel join forces—or rather allosauruses, to make up one complete creature to exhibit for profit at the Omaha State Fair—had been received first with incredulity, then interest and, finally, enthusiasm. "If a fake mermaid can make a man rich at a quarter a head to view it, just think what a real old dinosaur could rake in," Faro had said. The professors had thought about that and leaped at it.

With both men driving their workers on an around-the-clock effort, Fenn's skeletal fragments and Handel's jigsaw-puzzle of a skull had been coated with heavy protective and strengthening varnish, labeled and numbered, crated and transported by oxcart to the Missouri in record time, then flatboated downriver to Omaha. The presence of two noted academicians and a unique exhibit had so impressed the fair's commissioners that the professors and their allosaurus had been allotted a choice space. Now, with the fair's opening only a few days off, they were swarming over the rude construction that would shortly become a reasonable representation of the terrible reptile predator of 150 million years before and gloating over the prospect of taking in enough in admission fees to finance a fruitful completion to the summer's digging.

"Ought we not to have charged more, Fenn?" Handel called, securing a portion of rib to the burlap with a deft twist of baling wire. "That way, the money would accumulate at a more advantageous-to-ourselves rate."

"Better to keep the price low enough for everyone," Fenn said, eyeing a long bone he was holding with an air of indecision, then placing it among the lower ribs. "Better a hundred quarters than thirty half-dollars. Turnover's what you want in this game."

"They are learning pretty fast, for professors," Faro told Melissa Chapman.

"Indeed they are." She consulted her brooch watch. "It's close to five; maybe we'd best get back to Mrs. Limeburner's—dinner's at quarter to six."

"Good idea," Faro said. "This's been a long day, what with us getting here just this morning and everything getting settled and started setting up and all, and I am some hungry."

An hour later, Faro found that his appetite, if not diminished, was somewhat interfered with. The diner opposite him at the long table, whose head was two feet nearer the ceiling than Faro's, was a little distracting, but not so much so as the two on his left, who came to his shoulder only because they were perched on several books placed on their chair seats. A woman who seemed to feel that the best way to eat was with her right hand passed behind her neck so as to approach her mouth from the left side positively unnerved him. There were others he suspected might be worse, but they were on his side of the table and out of his direct vision.

Doc Prentiss had, years ago, recommended Mrs. Limeburner's theatrical boardinghouse as one of the best places to stay in Omaha. "Good food, and the company's varied," the old confidence man had said. "Touring actors, dancers, singers—always somebody interesting to talk to, my boy, and ladies more available than you might think. Any time you're in Omaha, go to Mrs. L., mention my name, and she'll squeeze you in, even though you're not, strictly speaking, a theatrical."

Faro had done so, and was beginning to regret it. The food and general comfort of the place was all Doc had said; but the theatricals now in residence, drawn by the fair, were more sideshow attractions than stage performers.

He looked across the table at Melissa Chapman, seated between the giant and the contortionist. She was talking animatedly to each and seemed to enjoy the company and the food.

"Takes getting used to, this kind of folk," the man next to him said. He at least seemed ordinary, to Faro's relief; about Faro's own age, with dark hair receding above the temples to form a widow's peak, and a long, sardonic, pale face. "But you don't want to be put off by the way they look or act," his neighbor went on. "They're grand people, making a living both in spite of and out of their peculiarities, and, I'll tell you, they know a lot more about living and caring and loyalty than most of the folks who pay to gawk at them."

"Some don't look too outlandish," Faro said. "Like that lady over there." The woman he indicated was not outstandingly pretty, ugly, tall, short, fat, thin nor, as far as could be seen, double-jointed nor bearded; she was dressed with a notable lack of flair in a brown dress whose neck covered half her throat.

"Ah, that's Geographia, the Living Map," his neighbor said. "Has all of the U.S. east of the Mississippi tattooed on her upper body in four colors, with Florida running down her left leg, all principal towns, cities and rail lines, rivers and canals. Keeps up to date with a visit to the tattooer every winter. It's hell on her when they change the name of a town, I'll tell you."

"She, uh, shows the whole territory?" Faro asked.

"Special tent, adult males only, admission six bits, for educational purposes," his neighbor said. "And so it is. I venture that no one who's ever seen Geographia will forget where Apalachee Bay is, nor Fort Wayne, Indiana and Johnstown, Pennsylvania." Faro, working out the rough location of these locales on the map and on Geographia's torso, had to agree that they would be memorable. He wondered what his neighbor's specialty was, but decided to wait until he chose to volunteer the information. Faro had lived a long time in parts where what would be friendly curiosity in a place like New York or Philadelphia tended to be taken as mortally offensive prying.

He reached out and speared a boiled potato from a dish in the middle of the table and deposited it on his plate in a puddle of gravy alongside a nicely browned piece of ham. He nearly dropped his fork as the potato said in a squeaky, almost mouse-like voice, "Damn! I hoped I'd be left over to get made up into potato cakes for breakfast. All right, don't mind me, just mash me up in the gravy and chomp me, and I hope I choke you."

He took a deep breath and turned to his neighbor. "Thought of asking you what you done for a living," he said, "but I see I don't got to. One of them voice-throwers, are you?"

"I was a professional ventriloquist once, yes," the man said, "and I like to keep my hand, or voice box, in now and then. But there wasn't much money in it. Now I do balloon ascensions at circuses and fairs—it's a great draw for them, don't you see, everybody hoping the gas in the balloon'll catch fire or the balloonist'll fall out of the basket and smash like an egg. I ought to attract a fair crowd here, being a home-town boy, Omaha-born—Oscar Diggs, at your service, sir."

Faro acknowledged the self-introduction and said,

"Faro Blake. In the gambling line, not the entertaining."

"And the lady who entered this establishment with you—would that be Mrs. Blake?"

"Not if she had her way, nor me neither, I guess," Faro said. "That is a Miss Chapman, which she is a writer for some magazine in the east, out here seeing how things is with the dinosaurs and Indians." He eyed his potato briefly and decided against eating it. After the protest Diggs had made it utter, it was a little like cannibalism.

"I wonder," Diggs said, "would you and Miss Chapman care to join me in an ascent, perhaps the one that opens the fair? As a journalist, she might like what I expect would be a unique experience, and a gambler such as yourself might relish the risk."

"I take risks in the way of business," Faro said. "They are less of a relish than something I got to put up with, like tight shoes on a long walk. So I don't admire to see if I get to be burned up or get my neck broke, just for the amusement of it." He turned back to the potato and began mashing it up, after all.

Mrs. Limeburner provided her boarders with tea or coffee and sweet biscuits after supper in her front parlor; and Faro, partaking of them, found himself in conversation with Geographia.

"I saw you were talking to that nice Mr. Diggs," she said. "He is a great friend to us people in the sideshow business. His pa was in politics here in Omaha, so he knows a lot of people here and in other places around. If there gets to be a problem with the local law, as sometimes happens, he is a wizard at getting it fixed up. Hardly any of don't owe him for some favor when we needed it."

"He is rising high in the world, it'd seem," Faro said.

"The ballooning, I mean. It seems some dangerous, but I guess it is a safer thing than the politics, all things considered."

As he made conversation, he found himself fascinated with the very ordinary woman before him. The drab dress gave no clear indication of whether her figure was lithe or only corseted, and there was nothing overtly attractive about her; but the knowledge Diggs had imparted to him of her surface decoration obsessed him. What would it be like, he wondered, to take a trip down the Ohio Valley? And damn, wouldn't marching through Georgia be something worth singing about. . . .

Geographia's company was claimed by some colleagues, and Melissa Chapman, carrying a cup of tea, joined him. "No, I will not go up in a balloon," she said, when he relayed Diggs's invitation to her. "I don't know how many times I've had people tell me, 'Women don't have both feet on the ground' when I've tried to show them I'm a serious professional person, and I don't propose to get both feet *off*."

"I ain't inclined to navigate the ocean of the air myself," Faro said. "What I got to get at, now that dinosaurs and professors and walking trips through the desert and all is maybe done with, is finding some of them people that has come into town with money to lose and taking enough of it off of them to stake me out in Jim McGaha's game in St. Louis, which is not far off getting under way."

"Is it all done with?" Melissa Chapman asked.

"There is some loose ends," Faro admitted. "I shot that Fowler, that shot at me, and I guess the Indians took care of them fellows that drug me off from camp. But there is still left open the question of who put Fowler and them up to it, and why. And since they didn't get the job done, I got to wonder, is there somebody, some place, that is set on punching my ticket to the hereafter? My experience, though, you keep moving and deny everything, most difficulties like that blow over."

Melissa Chapman regarded him with interest and amusement. "I think you may be a living disproof of Aristotle's dictum that the unexamined life is not worth living, Mr. Blake. On the other hand, is *your* life worth living?"

"I am breathing, and enjoying good food and drink when there's such to be had," he put in. "I line my pockets when I can and deal fair in what I do. If that ain't a life, what is it?"

"A good question," Melissa Chapman said. "Somehow, talking to you, I get a sense that life might be a huge joke—that, in fact, you might be right."

"If you want to discuss that some, later on," Faro said, "I believe we are about four doors apart, on the same side of the second-floor hall. I could maybe come in when everything's quiet, midnight or so, and we could have us a good talk about life and junk like that." In his experience, ladies who could be got into conversations about the Soul and the Larger Meaning of Life could be also pretty quickly got into bed.

"My door has a snap lock," Melissa Chapman said. "It wouldn't keep a determined intruder out very long; but long enough for me to fetch out the .32 revolver I keep under my pillow. Anybody who tries that door, I have to regard as a dangerous enemy and treat accordingly."

"Well, yes," Faro said. He still seemed like a long way from getting anywhere near where he wanted to be with Melissa Chapman. Maybe it was time and past time to be attending to his business.

*   *   *

Later that night, he had finished checking out the gambling establishments that Omaha afforded and chosen the Bucket of Blood as his base of operations. It was near to the fair grounds, and the proprietor hadn't been over greedy about his cut of Faro's proposed takings. Walking back toward Mrs. Limeburner's boardinghouse, he saw a familiar, bulky figure ahead of him in the street and hailed it: "Mr. Buckthorn!"

"Mr. Blake." Buckthorn greeted him and said, "It's a little surprising to find you here."

"Come no further than what you did," Faro said. "You in Omaha to take in the fair?"

"Not really," Buckthorn said. "There's a congressman from Pennsylvania here, and I want to see to it that he puts in a word to favor me for the Indian agent position back in the Dakotas. And with that backing, along with the rest that I have, I don't see how I can fail, do you, Mr. Blake?"

"Curious," Melissa Chapman said the next morning, listening to Faro's account of his meeting with Buckthorn.

"What way curious?" Faro asked. "That he's getting a congressman in his corner?"

"No," Melissa Chapman said. "That he'd make a point of telling you about it."

CHAPTER 14

The opening day of the Nebraska State Fair found Faro in an edgy mood. While the professors had been assembling their stellar attraction, and Melissa Chapman had been presumably gathering news and local color, he had been trying to build up his stake for Jim McGaha's game, now only a few days away. He had done well with his faro bank at the Bucket of Blood, but not yet well enough. He could be faced with getting into the game late but adequately financed, or at the beginning with not quite enough cash to feel secure, and it was hard to know which route to choose.

At Melissa Chapman's insistence, he subdued his uneasiness and joined her for a tour of the fairgrounds.

After they had watched a half-dozen yokels grappling with a greased pig, observed pens full of placid cattle, sheep and swine, been invited to chew on two new varieties of wheat, listened to a steam organ playing operatic airs and marches, taken in the sideshows featuring several of their fellow-boarders at Mrs. Limeburner's—with Faro alone, to Melissa Chapman's indignation, allowed to educate himself by studying Geographia's cartography—and consumed a consider-

141

able quantity of lemon phosphate, root beer and a kind of red sausage served on a bun, Faro was in a more cheerful frame of mind.

"We ain't never seen that allosaurus all put together," he told his companion. "Let's go give it a look."

At the professors' tent, they found Fenn standing on a box out front, haranguing the crowd. "The monster out of the past!" Harvard's Nebraska representative yelled. "More fearsome than the dragon Saint George slew, more frightful than Fafnir! See the creature that roamed the West a hundred and a half million years ago!"

"That would be a not-to-be-forgotten marvel," a man in the front of the crowd said. "I would give what I have to be able to see it."

"Not necessary, sir," Fenn said. "Merely the quarter of a dollar, two bits, five nickles, will gain you admission to this wonder of the ages. Thank you, sir, step right in." As Professor Handel paid his money and entered the tent, Faro wondered if the two academics had invented the concept of the shill on their own or had had some instruction.

The crowd surged up to pay the price of viewing Fenn's and Handel's reconstruction. There was a momentary halt in business when a tall, gaunt man wearing a broad-brimmed hat raised his arms skyward and shouted, "This is a snare of Satan! This monster that man is talking of ain't in the Book! There never was no such, not until that Darwin and his kind set themselves up to deny Holy Writ! Abandon hope, all ye who enter that there tent, for it's the mouth of the Hell that awaits unbelievers! The road to damnation and the eternal fire is paved with your quarters!"

Some potential customers seemed to take this exhortation to heart, and drifted away; but others, apparently figuring that a sniff at hellfire was worth a

quarter, pressed forward and urged their money on
Fenn. Faro wondered if the professors had hired this
Jeremiah to drum up trade, but decided that they were
not yet so sophisticated in their new work.

He handed over a half-dollar for himself and Melissa
Chapman, and entered the tent.

"Now, that is something," he said after a moment.
He had seen only fragments of the bones of the great
killer lizard, stuck seemingly at random onto the supporting form, before this. Now the whole creature was
in place and, even without life and flesh, seemed to
exude an air of implacable menace. About the height
of two men it rose above the earthen floor, a barrel-like
body balanced on two massive legs which terminated
in monstrous talons, with a heavy tail splayed out
behind it. The skull was pure nightmare, with hollow
eyepits seeming almost to hold the feral glare they had
had in life, and the terrible spiked jaws ajar as if to
rend and gulp. Even the seemingly useless forefeet
tucked up next to the chest added to the eerie horror;
they might have been meant to hold a napkin up in a
ghastly imitation of dainty table manners.

"It certainly is," Melissa Chapman said. "It's terrible,
but it's beautiful in a way, too—a creature that was
meant for one thing, and did it supremely well."

Hey, now, Faro told himself, there is one thing that
Miz Chapman likes, for once. Was I like some dinosaur,
I might could get somewheres with her. Then it occurred
to him that he fit her definition of beauty, being suited
for one function only, gambling, and doing that as well
as it could be done. It seemed to indicate that he had
a better chance at Melissa Chapman, but he wasn't
pleased at the comparison.

As they walked away from the tent, Handel and
Fenn caught up with them. "How come you closed up?"
Faro asked. "Doing a land-office business, looks like."

"We were and we will," Fenn said. "But right now, there's nothing doing. The balloon's about to go up, and none of the attractions'll draw any kind of crowd. So Handel and I, we figured we might as well go along and see it."

The four of them, spearheaded by Handel's capable elbows, worked their way through the crowd to a good vantage point from which to observe the half-inflated balloon that was heaving its way upward from the ground. Diggs stood in a wicker basket tethered to the balloon's lower end, waving to the crowd.

When the gas-making apparatus had finally filled the oiled-silk bag, it lifted, awkwardly at first, then more smoothly, finally hoisting the basket and its occupant from the ground. As it rose into the clear morning air, the crowd hurrahed and waved hats, caps and bonnets; a rapidly diminishing Diggs bowed over the edge of the basket and repeatedly gestured with his top hat.

The balloon seemed no larger than a pear, and the basket the size of a walnut, when it finally came to rest in the zenith, kept from rising further by the stout manila mooring line secured by the ground crew.

"He must be a thousand feet up," Fenn said, awed. "A fifth of a mile into the air. Handel," he went on, turning to his colleague, "could you *imagine* what that could do for us? If we could rise that high, d'you see how well we could make out the landscape? We could spot in a few moments the kind of good digging sites that it'd take us days to discover moving about on land."

"It would not be difficult," Handel agreed. "The ballon and basket are of simple construction. And the lifting power is hydrogen; a little calcium hydride and water is enough to produce all that is needed of that. I agree, it would greatly diminish the time and tedium of observation."

"Diggs'd be pleased to hear you say that," Faro said. "He is strong on ballooning, and doubtless he'd like to know that a brace of eminent men think it's got its uses."

"You know this aeronaut?" Handel asked.

"A fellow-boarder at Ma Limeburner's," Faro said. "Nice-spoke fellow, too."

The ground crew now began to haul on the ropes, and the balloon and its occupant began their descent.

"You must introduce us," Fenn said. "I want to find out more about this, what the whole business costs and what the problems are. Handel and I, we could steal a march on everybody else in paleontology if we took to the air. We'll buy him a drink."

"Lots of drinks," Handel said. "There is much dust in the air of your Nebraska."

Professor Handel's promise of lots of drinks held, and Faro had his share of them. His memory of the evening was vague after a while, but he recalled Diggs and the professors chatting animatedly about the problems and potentials of aerial observation. That he had not recalled everything was made clear late the next morning when Diggs, freshly shaven and offensively alert, shook him awake.

"You've missed breakfast, but that's all right," Diggs said. "I got Mrs. L. to save you some good hot coffee, and I expect that's all you'd probably want, your first time."

"First at what?" Faro wanted to know.

"Why, ballooning! You promised last night you'd go up with me today, said you wanted to see if the people on the ground really looked like ants, the way I said they did."

"That's what I wanted, was it?" Faro said dubiously.

"Said so. Well, come on. We're due to go up in half an hour."

"I expect I was joking when I said that," Faro said.

"Not the way you were talking," Diggs said. "Told everybody in the bar how you meant to go up into the clouds and didn't give a damn if you never came down again."

"I think that must of been rye whiskey they had at that bar," Faro said. "I don't believe I would of said something like that was I on bourbon. I said all that loud and public, huh?"

"Sure did. You'll want to put on an extra shirt or something; it gets kind of cold, up that high."

Faro sat up, winced and began reaching for the clothes on the chair next to his bed. Going a thousand feet up in the sky under a gas bag that might blow up or drop him to his death was not his idea of the way to start a day, or finish it either, for that matter. But he knew well enough that if he backed down on a publicly expressed intent, his credit as a gambler would suffer, making it even more difficult to do enough business to earn the stake for Jim McGaha's game. He forced himself to look on the positive side: the ascent would make him better-known, and maybe bring him more customers.

At the last moment, he was not so sure. The balloon, fully inflated, swayed above his head, and Diggs was already in the basket. The ground crew strained to hold the mooring rope taut enough to keep the basket against the ground from which it seemed ready to leap. As Faro approached it reluctantly, he stumbled over a rock in the ground.

A shrill voice called, "Pick me up, dunce!" Faro looked down and saw his knuckleduster-pistol lying on the ground, evidently jolted from his vest pocket by the impact of his stumble. "Come on, Blake!" the pistol said. "Poor old Diggs is waiting to take you up for the treat of your life."

Faro looked toward the balloon and its basket, only a few feet away. Diggs sketched a wave at him and grinned, then looked startled as the basket lurched and began to rise.

The ground crew stumbled backward at the release of the accustomed tension, and the dangling end of the mooring rope was visible beneath the ascending basket. One of the crew made a leap at it but missed; then suddenly the balloon was dwindling in the sky.

"Sumbitch just *broke*," the leader of the ground crew said. "Nothin' we could do about it."

The crowd gasped and shouted as the balloon continued upward, first to its height when tethered the day before, and then beyond. It drifted off to the north as it rose, and in a little while had vanished altogether. While it was still visible, it seemed to Faro that he could catch a hint of motion from the basket that might have been Diggs waving farewell with his tall hat.

Fenn came up to him and said, "I fear our friend is done for. If he can breathe the thin air at that height, likely he'll freeze to death. And if he doesn't, he'll probably come down in a wilderness where he'll starve, if he isn't dashed to pieces when it hits the ground. We won't see him again, that's for sure. Lucky you missed getting on."

Faro nodded slowly. He went over and looked at the rope that had so disastrously failed Diggs. It appeared to be frayed where it had given way, and some of it crumbled under its fingers as though it were rotten.

Faro had not known Diggs long, but he seemed to have been too thorough a man not to have checked the rope on which his life depended often enough to have spotted any rot setting in.

And a little acid dripped onto a rope would weaken

it in a few hours—in the time, say, since one Faro Blake had announced his intention of participating in that morning's ascent.

Maybe it was an accident, or maybe someone had it in for Diggs personally; but Faro doubted it. It was depressingly likely that whoever had hired Dirty Dave Fowler and his crew of thugs was still at large, and now operating in Omaha.

CHAPTER 15

The night of Diggs's aerial disappearance, Faro was beginning to think he might as well have shared the former ventriloquist's fate, for all the progress he was making in accumulating his stake for the McGaha game. The table at which he was running his faro bank at the Bucket of Blood was nicely crowded with customers who were dutifully losing two to five percent more than they won, thus enriching Faro comfortably if not spectacularly. But these model citizens were more than offset by a maverick player who bet erratically, seemingly on the inspiration of frequent pulls at a flask he carried in the pocket of his well-cut frock coat, usually managing to have his heaviest bet down on the winning card that slipped out of the dealing box. To add irritation to loss, he did not seem particularly to enjoy his winnings.

"More money," he said, raking in his latest stake and Faro's matching contribution. "Money's funny, money. Got to do all sorts things to get it sometimes, work for it, fight for it, sell soul for it and sometimes it just comes to you easy as you please."

"Sell soul?" Faro asked, dealing out the losing card

for the turn and noting sourly that, as usual, the man had not bet on it.

"She sells sea souls by the she sore," the man said carefully. "If I can say that right, I know I'm not drunk. Enough," he added, and refreshed himself from his flask. "Now, I'll put twenty on the seven . . . thank you, my good man." Faro paid off the bet on the winning card and raked in the losers' contributions. "And I'll copper twenty on the knave, fitting enough."

The jack of hearts was the losing card on that turn; and the flask-holder's placing of a copper token on his stake won him yet another portion of Faro's cash.

"Nice money, gambling money," the man said. "Not like some money, soul money, blood money."

Faro looked past the players and saw Simon Buckthorn enter the saloon. Buckthorn looked intently at Faro for a moment, as if debating whether to join in the game, then sketched a wave of greeting and left.

Three turns into the next game, with Faro's financial reserves being cut into by the erratic player's continual success, Melissa Chapman appeared at the table.

"Surprised to see you in a place like this," Faro said.

"It's about the only sort of establishment an unescorted woman can go to here," Melissa Chapman said. "They assume I'm a sporting lady, so they don't make any fuss, unlike the hotels and restaurants. My word," she said, turning to Faro's nemesis, who was now staring glassily at the green felt layout, "imagine meeting you here, Mr. Trimmer."

"I know you?" the man said.

"We met at President Hayes's inauguration two years ago," Melissa Chapman said. "I interviewed you about your new post as chairman of the House Committee on Indian Affairs. This is Representative Trimmer of Pennsylvania," she added, turning to Faro. "You're playing in distinguished company tonight."

"He is well named," Faro said gloomily. "He is trimming me for fair."

" 'S only money," Trimmer said. "Lots worse things to lose."

"I wonder if I could talk to you for a while, Congressman," Melissa Chapman said.

"Sure."

Faro was uncertain about whether to be indignant or relieved at Melissa Chapman's preemption of his disastrous customer.

"Last bet," Trimmer said. "You want to forget limit?" He emptied his pockets of his night's winnings, a substantial pile of coins and bills.

"Sure," Faro said heartily, quite aware that paying off would come close to wiping him out.

"On the trey, then." Trimmer shoved his stake onto the three of spades painted on the layout.

The winning card of the previous turn, still exposed in the dealing box, was the five of hearts. Faro slid it out, and exposed the loser for the next turn . . . the three of diamonds.

"Three of demons," Trimmer said cheerfully, as he watched Faro rake in everything the Congressman had won that night. "Now, ma'am, you want to talk? We'll go talk in corner, all right?" He lurched off to a vacant table.

As Melissa Chapman made to follow him, Faro said, "This Trimmer fellow is likely the one that Buckthorn was looking to meet up with to talk about that agent job he's after. Maybe you could put in a good word for him, if Trimmer's in any shape to understand it."

"I'll be asking questions, not giving recommendations," Melissa Chapman said.

Over the next quarter of an hour, as he dealt and, usually, won, Faro noticed from time to time that Congressman Trimmer and Melissa Chapman were deep in conversation. The next time he looked up, they were gone.

Not much after that, he closed his game for the night. There were only a few quarter and four-bit players left, and, on Trimmer's last bet, he had won enough to put him within striking distance of his needed stake. Another couple of even ordinary days in fair-time Omaha, and he would have what it took to get into Jim McGaha's game and could book passage downriver to St. Louis.

Outside, in the darkened street, he turned toward Mrs. Limeburner's boardinghouse. Ahead of him he made out, silhouetted by a distant street lamp, the figure of a woman. He quickened his pace to catch up with her. Alone, in the street, at this hour, it wasn't hard to tell what she was, and he felt elated enough by the final result of the evening's play to want what she might have to offer, or sell.

"Evening," Faro said, falling into step beside her.

"Good evening, Mr. Blake."

"I, uh, wondered whereat you went to after you left the place back there," Faro said, rapidly revising his intentions.

"I managed to walk the Congressman back to his hotel," Melissa Chapman said. "Lurch him back would be more accurate, I suppose."

"He did seem pretty far gone," Faro agreed. "Get anything that made sense out of him in your talk?"

"Some. Perhaps enough."

"Able to do any good for Buckthorn?"

"The congressman is aware of Mr. Buckthorn's qualifications," Melissa Chapman said.

"Get anything out of Trimmer that'd be good for your magazine?"

"Possibly."

It seemed to Faro that every question he asked got a

polite answer that effectively cut off further conversation. He began to feel irritated. After all, he had something to celebrate, and he was walking and talking with a personable woman. It would be nice at least to have a lively conversation with her, if nothing more.

"Been in Omaha before, have you?"

"No."

"But you was in Washington, I think you said, for the inauguration?"

"Yes."

"That must have been some doings."

"It was."

They were almost to the Limeburner establishment now, and Faro was seething with frustration. Damn the woman anyhow—she might be preoccupied with her work or whatever, but that was no excuse to go on cutting him off. There was one question, anyhow, that would get more than a yes or no or other short answer out of her, and he felt sore enough to try it.

"Care to go to bed with me?"

"Yes."

He stopped, jolted. "What I said was—"

"I heard you. Yes. You asked, I answered. We'll go to your room."

Melissa Chapman placed her neatly folded camisole and drawers on top of her neatly folded serge dress on the oak chair in Faro's room, next to which her neatly aligned shoes stood, and turned to face him. His own clothes were in a tangled heap beside the bed, and he hoped she would not insist on his straightening them out before they got down to the night's work.

She was lean but full-bosomed, sturdier-thighed than he would have expected. His reverie on the Deadwood stage had been inaccurate in one respect; her nipples were not pale rose, but deep red, and they were promisingly erect.

She reached out and stroked his erection, then gripped it firmly. "Very nice," she said.

Faro thrust a hand between her legs and sent a finger probing warmth and moisture. "That is pretty good, too."

They stood silently for a moment, Faro's hand and Melissa Chapman's both moving with increasing intensity.

"Listen," he finally said hoarsely, "this is great, but we could get the whole thing over with just standing here like this, and that'd be a waste."

"So it would," she said. They fell onto the bed, Faro sprawling over Melissa Chapman. She wriggled from under him with a frantic motion.

"You want to be on top?" he said.

She shook her head. "Neither one. Side by side."

As they faced each other on the bed, she raised one leg and he eased himself into her. She closed her eyes briefly, then reopened them to look at him intently, as he flexed himself to thrust, recoil and thrust again. "Slowly," she said. She drew one of his hands to her breast and pressed it against the springy nipple. She left his hand there and sent her own down to where they were joined, girdling his erection with tight fingers and churning it against her yielding flesh. It was less active than he was used to, but intensely erotic, and, sooner than expected, he was at the point of climax.

Then Melissa Chapman's right hand was cupping his testicles and her left forefinger was doing something astonishing a few inches behind them, and he jerked like a hooked trout, exploding inside her.

"Well, hey," he said after a while, as they lay side by side on the rumpled coverlet, "I would not of expected anything like this, recalling that ramble we took under the stars out at old Fenn's diggings. I mean, you was pretty standoffish then."

"I don't like indirection," Melissa Chapman said. "Stars and sly talk, and sliding your hand where you could claim it was just a mistake, that kind of school-boy silliness puts me off. If a man wants to go to bed with a woman, he ought to say so, just as you did tonight. She can say yes or she can say no. Either way, it's honester than all the seduction ritual. What this wants—" she grasped his relaxed penis "—is the same thing as what this wants." She pulled his hand between her thighs. "Sometimes it just won't do for a particular man and woman, sometimes it will; but the main thing is to be honest about what it is you want."

"What I would want now," Faro said, "is a puff or so at a good cigar whilst I get my faculties restored, and then do some more of what we just done. That okay with you?"

"Yes," Melissa Chapman said.

Faro scratched a match to sputtering life on the floor-boards, but before he could touch it to his cigar, the door to his room was kicked open and a horde of people ranging in height from two feet six to eight feet plunged in and began raining blows on him.

CHAPTER 16

Melissa Chapman gave a shriek like a locomotive's whistle, and scrambled to the top edge of the bed.

Faro slid to the floor and found himself face to face with one of his attackers, the dwarf who usually sat opposite him at the evening meal. The little man hit him in the face and cursed him vilely. Faro scrambled away, and was pinned in the corner of the room by the woman contortionist, who managed to get a strangling arm around his neck, although she was facing away from him. His bulging eyes registered the baleful presence of Geographia, her cotton wrapper, gaping at the top, revealing most of the Great Lakes and part of Chicago.

He eeled away from the contortionist's grip, and fought off the impassioned assault of the second dwarf, with some idea of making for the door. He was hampered both by his nakedness and by his unwillingness to hit out hard at the little men or the women. He lost this second compunction when the giant hit him a massive blow on top of the head that seemed to him as if it would drive him through the floor. He shook his head, drew back his right fist, and cut loose with what, faced with a standard opponent, would have been a killing uppercut to the jaw. It took the giant somewhere below the breastbone, and the eight-footer folded to the floor with a whistling gasp, his eyes rolled up, unconscious before he slammed into the planks.

"You people!" Melissa Chapman's yell focused all eyes on her; her appearance stopped hostilities for the moment. Splendidly naked, she stood at the head of the bed, glaring at them, her hair loosely tumbled and her breasts quivering with fury.

"What the hell is this all about?" she said.

"He done for poor old Oz Diggs," Geographia said. "Cut the rope on's balloon and left him to drift off to a lonely death. Oz was a friend to us all, and we don't propose to see the man that killed him get away with it."

"Who told you that?" Melissa Chapman asked.

"Harold, there," Geographia said, pointing to the recumbent giant. "Came back about an hour ago all fired up—someone told him how it was, he said, and said we should go show Blake what Oz's friends were made of."

"I can see there's no use asking Harold just yet about who told him what," Melissa Chapman said, "but I will tell you that he's got it all wrong. Mr. Blake as near as anything went up in that balloon with Mr. Diggs, and he had nothing to do with the rope breaking. I was there and I saw it all. And, good gracious," she went on, "whatever would Mr. Blake want to harm Mr. Diggs for? They just met the other day. You can tell by looking at him that Mr. Blake isn't the kind of man to do that." The invading sideshow folk looked at Faro, who shuffled his bare feet uneasily. Not in his wildest dreams had he pictured himself naked, and being inspected by two dwarves, a contortionist and a tattooed lady to see if he seemed capable of murdering a man by setting him adrift in a balloon.

"Harold seemed sure of it," the contortionist said.

"Well, then, you'll have to ask Harold some questions when he wakes up," Melissa Chapman said. "Why don't you just get him and yourselves out of here and leave me and Mr. Blake to . . . leave us alone?"

Confused and ill at ease, the sideshow people departed, pushing Harold along the floor. Faro aided them with the massive legs until the giant was through the doorway, then shut the door.

"I hope Harold's room is on this floor," he said. "It don't do to think of the job they would have getting him downstairs. What the hell was all that about, do you suppose?"

He had expected no answer to this puzzle from Melissa Chapman; but, glancing at her, he caught an expression of thoughtful knowledge on her face. "Hey, you know something about this," he said.

"Not know," Melissa Chapman said.

"But you got some thoughts? What are they, if you don't mind saying?"

"If I have thoughts," Melissa Chapman said, "I'm going to keep them to myself for a while. It's important to me, you know, to find a big story out here, and I think I've got one. It could spoil it if I were to talk about some of the details before it's time."

"Well, hell, yeah, sure," Faro said. "I can see where that story is more important to you than my ass is to me, so I can't hardly complain, can I? I been shot at, kidnaped, near ballooned to death and set on by a bunch of sideshow people, but that ain't nothing alongside of you getting a story out of it. Jesus!"

Melissa Chapman sank to a sitting position on the bed, her legs splayed comfortably. "You have a right to be angry with me," she said.

"Well, and so I am," Faro said indignantly.

"Are you sure?"

He followed the direction of her gaze and saw that his penis, without any conscious attention on his part, had risen and was pointing at her. "Well, maybe not furious," he said. "But mad enough so I'll be on top this time."

"That's fine with me," Melissa Chapman said, and let her legs open invitingly.

Faro's entry this time had the force of his anger and the restraint of the wariness he had begun to feel; but as he slid into Melissa Chapman's warm enfoldment, his hostility began to dissolve in a succession of rhythmic thrusts.

Beneath him, she suddenly stiffened and glared—not at him but past him.

"*Es tut mir leid.*"

"I *do* beg your pardon."

Faro groaned inwardly and looked over his shoulder. Fenn and Handel stood in the room's doorway. Maybe Chapman and me ought to hire a tent on the fairgrounds for our humping, he thought. Just as many folks'd be watching, but at least we'd get to charge admission.

CHAPTER 17

The two professors remained silent until Melissa Chapman, icily furious, had resumed her clothing and stamped out of the room. Faro wrapped himself in the coverlet and lit the cigar he had almost started on before the irruption of Harold and his friends, which seemed like a long time ago now.

"I am sorry," Handel ventured after Faro had glowered at them for a moment through the cloud of cigar smoke. "We had no idea that you would be occupied at this hour."

"Well, I ain't now, nor likely to be in the same style for some time," Faro said. "Miz Chapman don't take kindly to being put on display for the passing throng, and I don't know that I'm so set on it neither."

"It is a matter of urgency," Handel said.

"As my own urgencies ain't about to be met, I guess I might as well hear yours," Faro said.

Fenn and Handel, it appeared from their account, had been at the Grand Union saloon, discussing the day's takings and some new wrinkles to draw the crowd, when they had been joined by Simon Buckthorn, with ominous news.

"You remember that fellow you saw at the tent this morning?" Fenn asked. "The one that was going on about damnation and Darwin? As bad as that man back in Deadwood, that called me a blasphemer. Well, it seems as though he's been stirring up people in town about it. Buckthorn says there's a bunch of them that are in an ugly mood and that there's talk of coming out and breaking up the allosaurus skeleton. Now, we can't have that happen. It would be a tragic loss to science."

"And we took in more than three hundred dollars today," Handel said.

"One way and another, I can see you'd be anxious," Faro said.

"So it needs to be guarded, d'you see?" Fenn said.

"And you fellows decided you ain't the guarding type," Faro said. "That it?"

"If you would be so kind," Handel said.

"Why the hell not? I don't figure on getting any more sleep tonight anyhow. Wasn't for this, I'd just be lying here and cursing steady and mean-like."

Faro pulled his clothes on, secured his cut-down shotgun from his tool case, checked to make sure both barrels were loaded and left the boardinghouse for the fairgrounds.

As he made his way through the early-morning streets of Omaha, his mood lightened. He had, after all, not had such a bad evening. Congressman Trimmer had supplied him with the greater part of what he needed for the McGaha game, and Melissa Chapman had gone a good way toward meeting some other needs. It was galling to have been interrupted, but losing a second shot was a good deal less trying than stopping with a full load. And there would still be a good deal more territory to explore with Melissa Chapman. She had a kind of independence that could make for some interesting and inventive humping, for certain.

At the fairgrounds, he picked his way among the silent tents until he located allosaurus's quarters. Everything was silent except for the occasional muttered complaint from the prize hogs penned up some distance away.

Faro slipped into the tent, found a lantern, levered the chimney up and struck a match to the wick. In the dim light, the wired skeleton loomed, huger and more menacing than in the daylight.

Faro wondered what had once covered those bones. Was the skin pebbly and bright-colored, like some of the desert lizards he had seen? It would have been something to have seen it back then, alive and racing after you with murder in its heart—or rather its belly. The thing was a killing machine, clearly, made to satisfy its appetite and do nothing else in the world. He unlimbered the shotgun from its sling under his coat and laid it on the table Fenn used to take tickets, now deposited inside the tent. He wondered how much there was to Buckthorn's alarm about the mob of enraged Biblical literalists. Not much, he decided. Some of those people could work themselves up into a fury over drinking, gambling, fornication or the success of a competing denomination, but he couldn't see them doing more about something as remote as old stone bones than yell.

Faro studied the gigantic fanged skull, supported by a pole stuck into the ground, and wondered if the Scripture enthusiasts honestly believed that the two professors had somehow constructed the whole thing to delude the faithful.

The hair on the back of his neck rose, and he suddenly changed his opinion about the likelihood of intruders. There was a stir in the shadows at the rear of the tent, a rustle of canvas and the sure sense of another presence. He reached for the shotgun.

"Don't try it, Blake." Faro snatched the weapon up and turned to aim it toward the voice from the darkness. He heard the crash of a shot at the same time as something hit the shotgun with the force of a hammer blow and wrenched it from his hand with a spark of metal striking metal before he could fire it.

He launched himself, low to the ground, in the direction from which the shot had come, saw a shadowed figure, and made a brief grab at a trousered leg before a slamming blow took him behind the left ear and sent him sprawling and dazed to the dirt floor of the tent.

On hands and knees, dazed, he looked up to confront the man who had slugged him.

"You've been after me a long while, Blake," Simon Buckthorn said. "Now you've got me to yourself. I don't know how much you're going to enjoy it. Or how long."

CHAPTER 18

"Why would I be after you?" Faro said, gauging whether a leap at Buckthorn would be a long chance or no chance at all, and deciding that for the moment the odds were too great. "All I know about you is you want to be a Indian agent, and more power to you."

"And, of course, you admire me as an idealist who wants to take care of the poor, downtrodden red man," Buckthorn said with heavy irony.

"That was about the picture I had," Faro said cautiously.

Buckthorn snorted. "You and that Chapman bitch," he said. "Both of you, snooping, pretending to believe that shit, and closing in on me. She's better at it than you are, Blake. I don't know who you're working for— is it the Dakota Territorial government, maybe Indian Affairs in Washington?—but they aren't getting their money's worth. You gave yourself away with that comment about vaccination back in Deadwood, and then running off with my woman cinched it."

Faro rummaged through his recollection and came up with a feeble joke about getting a vaccination against gambling, which left him none the wiser. "Now," he protested, "that Mehitabel, first, I had no notion she was whatever to you, and second, it was her took the notion of running, and me into it only by way of accommodation, as she seemed frighted about something. Oh. That'd be you, I guess."

"You don't have to guess," Buckthorn said, "you damned well know. You wouldn't have said what you did, or cottoned onto Mehitabel, if you hadn't."

Faro decided that it would be no good explaining that he had a tendency toward humorous comment that didn't always strike everyone as funny, and that, like any man, he got horny at times and would satisfy that horniness with a convenient woman and even recognize afterward that he had some obligation to help her if she was in distress.

"Once you got to Mehitabel, you had to know about the blankets and the smallpox," Buckthorn said. "And that was the important part. That and Meyner and his crowd. The rest, the swindling, the arrangements for splitting the government allotments, that's ordinary enough so that it wouldn't have raised any fuss that mattered—Trimmer could have handled that easily enough."

"Heydee," Faro said tonelessly, recalling an old Indian's lament for his dead people out in the Badlands, "you are figuring to work the old Mandan stuff, once you get the agenting appointment? Hand out blankets infected with smallpox so's the most of 'em get sick and die?"

"As you well know, obviously," Buckthorn said. "What's left of them will be meat for Meyner and some of the others who think like him. A smallpox epidemic and a few more Crow Creeks, and there won't be any Indian question left to bother opening up this whole part of the country. There's men in Congress and in the War Department behind this, because they believe in it, and others, like Trimmer, that have been bought. The agent that's in there now is only out for money, so a man like me is needed—someone who's up to doing a job of extermination. I would admire to know," he went on, looking hard at Faro, "just who you're with, what kind of white men would set themselves up against doing what has to be done."

"I ain't in with nobody," Faro said. "I am a man in the gambling trade and nothing else. You have got hold of the wrong end of the stick, Buckthorn. Say, now, is it you I got to thank for sending Fowler and them after me?"

"When you went off with Mehitabel, it was plain that you were onto me, and up to some strange game by hiding out with Fenn—so it seemed best to eliminate you both. When I learned that didn't work, and that you'd turned up here, I made it my business to see that you didn't get any further. You should have been in that balloon this morning, you know—but, since you weren't, I dropped a couple of words in the ear of that shambling oaf of a giant—figured those freaks would do for you. Those were all good plans, damn it, but none of them came off." Buckthorn brooded for a moment, though never letting his pistol waver from its bead on Faro's forehead.

"Then you got the professors het up about the Bible-thumpers figuring to unravel old all-sorts here, so as to—"

"Get you out where I could deal with you, right. You're a shrewd adversary, Blake, and I don't suppose I'll ever know all that you've been up to."

"*I* don't suppose I could make you understand that you got it all wrong?" Faro said. "Like I was just in Deadwood trying to make a stake to get into Jim Mc-Gaha's big poker game down in St. Louis and said what I done about vaccination in the way of a joke and that the Mehitabel business hadn't nothing to do with you, so far as I knew, and me talking to that congressman was along of him winning a bunch of money from me and then losing it all back? It don't make that much of a story that way, but it's what happened."

"Well, now," Buckthorn said reflectively. "It could be that way, now couldn't it? I am big enough to admit it when I make a mistake, I hope. It would be pretty funny, wouldn't it, if I went to all that trouble for nothing?"

"If there is a saloon still open, maybe we could go there and buy each other a drink and have us a laugh about that," Faro said warily.

Buckthorn shook his head. "I might have been wrong about your nosing around my affairs, I'll allow that. But I've just now told you everything about them, haven't I? So, either way, you're too dangerous to me to be allowed to talk. You die here and now, and that Chapman woman goes next—whatever you are or aren't, she's a clear and present danger. She's talked to Meyner's men and to that fool Trimmer who doesn't have the stomach to stay bought when he's paid for. If I can work it out to get her off some place, she won't die easily, either."

Faro's jaw dropped, his eyes widened, and he gave a shrill scream as of a man in mortal fear. "Christ almighty!" he yelled. "The goddamned old lizard's come to life! Run or he'll get you!"

For an instant only the pistol wavered as Buckthorn, shaken by Faro's vivid feigning of a horror beyond normal experience, glanced at the wired-together allosaurus skeleton; but the instant was all that Faro had hoped to buy. He dove for Buckthorn's knees, made contact, and sent him reeling away.

"Now, Blake!" Buckthorn called as, still stumbling backward, he raised the pistol. He hit the post supporting the ancient reptile's massive skull and displaced it.

Faro threw himself to one side as Buckthorn triggered a shot that snarled above him, and knew with a sick hopelessness that he could not dodge the next one.

It did not come. Quickly in real time, nightmare-slow to Faro, allosaurus's skull, deprived of its support, fell. One pickaxe-sized fang entered Buckthorn's neatly barbered head at the center of his scalp and sank in to half its length. An instant later, Buckthorn lay under the shattered fragments of the skull, his pistol resting a foot from his unmoving fingers.

CHAPTER 19

Faro stood up and brushed some fragments of powdered stone from his clothing. The portion of allosaurus's skull that had not been cushioned by Buckthorn's body had virtually exploded on impact with the hard-packed earth, spraying the area with its remnants.

"That is going to be something for them two professors to put back together again," he muttered, feeling light-headed with his sudden escape from death. "Humpty Dumpty just ain't in that class, my, no." Laughter bubbled in his throat, but he suppressed it, sensing that it might go on and on if it began. Buckthorn was so funny-looking, with that big spike of a tooth through the top of his head, and the rest of him kind of mashed underneath the remaining portion of the old lizard's skull, and the ground around him darkening as it soaked up what the ruin of his body yielded.

Faro made his way to the edge of the tent, pausing to pick up his shotgun and return it to its sling. He turned and looked back at the mounted skeleton. Even headless, it had a monstrous majesty. Well, old lizard, he said silently, you really done something tonight. A hundred and fifty million years dead, and you got yourself your last game with one bite. You could put that in the record book, if lizards kept such.

He let himself out of the tent, putting together the story he would have to tell. Any suggestion that he and Buckthorn had had an argument which had ended in Buckthorn's death would be a bad idea, resulting at best in protracted legal proceedings which would keep him in Omaha, if not in the Nebraska state prison, until long past the finish of Jim McGaha's game.

He had, he decided, come into the tent to find poor Buckthorn in his present sorry state. Perhaps Buckthorn had gone there to protect the paleontological marvel from the hordes of irate believers he had warned Fenn and Handel of, and met his end in a valiant struggle with them; perhaps he had, overcome by early religious convictions, made his own attempt to destroy the satanic symbol. In either case, the point to be clear on was that he was well and truly dead before Faro Blake, of no fixed address, entered on the premises.

There was the problem of the two shots Buckthorn had fired, but they seemed to have aroused no attention so far, and the only witnesses to where and when they had been fired were some wakeful pigs, whose testimony, even if called for, would not carry much weight.

With his own problems satisfactorily disposed of, Faro felt a slight pang when he thought of the dilemma the professors faced in the morning. Their star attraction was now headless, and he estimated that it would take weeks of work, and a lot of plaster of Paris, before they would have a displayable skull back together; and by then the fair would be over.

Maybe, he thought, they could embalm Buckthorn and put him on show, with the allosaurus tooth still in him. That would be a draw, for sure, the Monster's Last Victim. And it would be fitting enough; Buckthorn had turned out to have about the same instincts as the old murdering reptile.

So, first thing in the morning, a report to the police and the professors. And second thing in the morning, a little talk with Melissa Chapman. The lady had to have known a lot more about Buckthorn and the whole situation than she had let on to Faro Blake, even after Faro Blake had got about as familiar with her as a man could, and concealing that knowledge had come close to making Faro Blake the late Faro Blake. He would have a few choice words to address to her, all right.

What he actually said, finding her in his bed as he entered his room, was "Hey."

"I came back," she said.

"And now so've I," Faro said, sitting on the chair and slipping his boots off.

"I was mad, but I saw that there wasn't any reason to be angry with you."

"No, there wasn't." His coat, shirt and trousers were on the floor now, and he was pulling down his drawers. There were about a dozen complaints he could make to her, but they seemed beside the point right now, with her there, mostly outside the covers and glistening in the lamplight. Even old allosaurus, cold blood and all, would have seen what came first.